Vinegar Street

Philip Ridley was born in the East End of London, where he still lives and works. He studied painting at St Martin's School of Art and by the time he graduated had exhibited widely throughout Europe and written his first novel. As well as three books for ned screenplay for *The Krays* three successful adult stage p *The Fastest Clock in the Unive* ace, and three for young peop and *Brokenville*. He has also directed two films from his own screenplays: *The Reflecting Skin* – winner of eleven international awards – and *The Passion of Darkly Noon*. Philip Ridley has written nine other books for children: *Mercedes Ice, Dakota of the White Flats, Krindlekrax* (winner of the Smarties Prize and the W. H. Smith Mind-Boggling Books Award), *Meteorite Spoon, Kasper in the Glitter* (nominated for the 1995 Whitbread Children's Book Award), *Dreamboat Zing, The Hooligan's Shampoo, Scribbleboy* (which received a commendation at the NASEN Special Educational Needs Children's Book Awards 1997 and was shortlisted for the Carnegie Medal) and *ZinderZunder*.

Stephen Lee was born in Ilford, Essex in 1957. He studied Art and Graphics at Walthamstowe College, but went on to become involved in social work, particularly with children. Several years later he became a freelance illustrator, and made a reputation for himself producing political illustrations. Stephen then moved into the general publishing market and his work can often be seen on book covers and inside illustrations. His interests include sport and travel.

Philip Ridley

Vinegar Street

Illustrated by Stephen Lee

PUFFIN BOOKS

PUFFIN BOOKS

Published by the Penguin Group
Penguin Books Ltd, 27 Wrights Lane, London W8 5TZ, England
Penguin Putnam Inc., 375 Hudson Street, New York, New York 10014, USA
Penguin Books Australia Ltd, Ringwood, Victoria, Australia
Penguin Books Canada Ltd, 10 Alcorn Avenue, Toronto, Ontario, Canada M4V 3B2
Penguin Books (NZ) Ltd, 182–190 Wairau Road, Auckland 10, New Zealand

On the World Wide Web at: www.penguin.com

Penguin Books Ltd, Registered Offices: Harmondsworth, Middlesex, England

First published 2000
1 3 5 7 9 10 8 6 4 2

Text copyright © Philip Ridley, 2000
Illustrations copyright © Stephen Lee, 2000
All rights reserved

The moral right of the author and illustrator has been asserted

Typeset in Palatino

Made and printed in England by Clays Ltd, St Ives plc

British Library Cataloguing in Publication Data
A CIP catalogue record for this book is available from the British Library

ISBN 0–140–38509–6

For Justin Ward –
who hears the same music

Prologue

Broken glass!

Doll's arm!

Tin can!

Poppy puts the objects in her black handbag and thinks, What beautiful treasure!

Poppy Picklesticks is twelve years, six months and twenty days old (Poppy likes to be precise about things). She is tall – some would say lanky – and so pale that, if you didn't know better, you'd send her to the doctor for a tonic. Her eyes are large and dark, and her stare – if you've never seen it before – can be quite alarming.

But here – here, on Vinegar Street – nothing about Poppy alarms anyone. No one bats an eyelid at her ankle-length black dress (decorated with a pattern of white skulls) or her long silk gloves (black, naturally) or her hair (very long, very straight and very black). And as for her shoes (the clumpiest, highest and – you've guessed it! – blackest platforms you've ever seen) . . . well, amongst the rubble and weeds of Vinegar Street, Poppy fits in just fine –

Something's coming!

Poppy stands bolt upright and stares into the distance.

Sometimes she gets this feeling – like a tingling voice inside her – and, although she can't explain it, this voice is always right –

A car!

No one ever comes to Vinegar Street, thinks Poppy. It's

in the middle of nowhere. And yet – there! A dark spot. Trembling in the summer's heat. Getting closer and closer and closer –

It's Mr Harmony!

Mr Harmony! Poppy hasn't seen him for . . . oh, it must be one year, two months and six days. Mr Harmony was responsible for building Vinegar Street. His sales brochure had declared: 'Bargain homes surrounded by a beautiful

landscape with a river full of wildlife.' But, in reality, should have read: 'Shoddily built slums, surrounded by a vast, muddy wilderness, with a canal full of chemical waste (from a nearby Nuclear Power Plant, no less).'

As a result, as soon as anyone moved in, they shrieked in horror and moved out again. Of the seven Harmony Homes originally built, three fell down (Nos. 2, 3 and 4) and another (No. 7 – the last to be built) has never been lived in –

Ka-chug!

Mr Harmony's car splutters to a halt.

Look at him! thinks Poppy. Still twitching and flinching. And I do believe he's plumper and balder. And as for his suit . . . well, it seems to consist entirely of stains, sweat and creases.

'Greetings, Mr Harmony,' calls Poppy, clambering out of the weeds and striding – some would say clumping – over to the car. 'A pleasure to see you again.'

'Stop that sarcasm right now!'

'But I'm not being sarc–'

'I'm a sick man! Guess what I've got a stomach full of?'

'Bacon sandwiches?'

'Ulcers!'

'Stress causes ulcers, Mr Harmony.'

'You bet your sweet patootie it's stress! I tell you, an astronaut stranded in space with a comet heading straight for him and with ants in his pants – which, of course, he can't scratch – is leading a life of blissful tranquillity compared to me. My nerves are frayed thinner than an Egyptian mummy's feet after it's boogied all night in the Dance-Till-You-Drop Disco. And you know why? This place! Vinegar Street! I'm sorry I ever built it.'

'But it's paradise, Mr Harmony.'

'More sarcasm! My ulcers will burst in a minute!'

Mr Harmony takes a tin of paint and a brush from the

boot of his car. Then he goes up to the 'FOR SALE' sign
outside No. 7.
    He's . . . he's writing something on the sign.
    Now he's rushing back to the car.
    Puts the paint and brush back in the boot and –
    SLAM!

– gets in the car and –
'Farewell, Mr Harmony!'
'Stop that sarcasm!'
– drives away.
For a moment everything is still.
Just the sound of insects . . .
Then –
Poppy strides over to the 'FOR SALE' sign.
'Mercy me!' she gasps out loud.
For there, in dribbling black paint, is the single word:

— PART ONE —

TingleVoice

— 1 —

'Sold, ya say?'

'Sold, Auntie Bruiser!'

'Well, what d'ya know? Where's that oily rag got to?'

'Behind you, Auntie Bruiser.'

Bruiser is in her back garden surrounded by the two hundred and twenty-three pieces of machinery that, when fitted together, form her beloved motorbike. She's been attempting this re-assembly for three hours and ten minutes, so, needless to say, she's covered in grease: it's smeared across her face and through her closely cropped hair. Her T-shirt is covered with handprints and the muscles in her arms – oh, yes, motorbiking has given her a physique most body-builders would envy – are gleaming with the stuff. Fortunately, her leather trousers (with tassles down the sides) and boots (covered with so many buckles they clink like spurs) are black already, so the grease blends in just nicely.

'You don't seem very interested, Auntie Bruiser.'

'Wh . . . what's that, DeputyPops?'

'No. 7!' exclaims Poppy, sitting on a slab of concrete. 'The house that's been empty since the very beginning – yeah, verily, since the book of Genesis – is soon to be most *un*empty. Boards taken off windows. Door unlocked. In short, sold! Sold! With everything that entails, Auntie Bruiser. New voices! New people! In short, new neighbours! Mercy me, if this ain't the most gobsmacking event since Moses looked at the Red Sea and said, "A neat parting, if you please", then I don't know what is. And what do *you* do? Ask about oily rags!'

'Oh, I'm darned sure it's important news, DeputyPops,' sighs Bruiser, removing her red neckerchief and dabbing sweat from her forehead. 'And I'm mighty grateful to you for delivering it. But : . . . well, my mind's on other things at the moment. You see, I'm afraid I'm gonna have to put Old Gal out of her misery.'

Old Gal is what Bruiser calls her motorbike. She bought it twelve years, six months and twenty-seven days ago and – if truth be told – it was second-hand and hardly in top-notch condition even then. But, over the past few months, it's been giving Auntie Bruiser no end of grief. Hardly a day's gone by without something falling off or leaking or, worse still, conking out altogether.

'There's . . . no hope at all?' asks Poppy, gently.

'None,' replies Bruiser, plonking herself next to Poppy. 'Kindest thing is to let Old Gal go peaceful-like.' She brushes a tear from her eye. 'Sure will miss her, though.'

I hate to see Auntie Bruiser upset like this, thinks Poppy. I wish I could do something to help. Wait! I've got an idea –

'A funeral, Auntie Bruiser!'

'Wh . : . what d'ya mean, DeputyPops?'

'A funeral! Mercy me, yes. A proper sending off for the Old Gal. Why not? After all, I've known her all my life. She's always been a good friend. We've got to say goodbye properly, Auntie Bruiser. We'll bury her right here – the back garden of No. 6 will be her eternal resting place. You'd like that, wouldn't you?'

'Wobbling wagonwheels!' exclaims Bruiser, giving Poppy a squeeze. 'Only you could have such a darned idea. Bless your hide, I'd like it very much.'

'How does tomorrow afternoon sound?'

'Saddle sores 'n' spur blisters – sounds just perfect.'

'I'll get organizing immediately, Auntie Bruiser.'

'Thanking you kindly, DeputyPops. And . . . well, about those new neighbours. You mustn't worry your little head about it.'

'But . . . I'm not worried, Auntie Bruiser.'

'Well, you look it, DeputyPops.'

'Well . . . I'm not.'

You sure?

. . . Yes.

You should be!

Why?

You'll find out!

— 2 —

'A . . . *what*, Poppyducks?'

'Funeral, Uncle Larry.'

'For . . . Old Gal?'

'Correct.'

'Oh, how unutterably riff-raff!'

Uncle Larry is tall and slim – some would say skinny – with balding hair, streaked with grey. He's wearing pinstripe trousers, slippers, a white shirt (open at the neck to reveal a cravat) and a long, flowing dressing gown decorated with oriental dragons. Now, if all this sounds a little posh and pricey, don't be fooled. Nothing could be further from the truth. Most of the clothes are either very old or second-hand (or, in the case of the dressing gown, both), and in need of a good scrub.

'A toast!' declares Larry, jumping from the sofa and dashing to the cocktail cabinet.

'To what, Uncle Larry?'

'Why, to your spiffing riff-raff imagination, Poppyducks.' He starts splashing various drinks into a cocktail shaker. 'Oh, hoity-toity folk ain't got any imagination at all. That's why I gave up my posh manor house. Did I ever tell you I used to be posh, Poppyducks?'

'Two thousand and thirteen times, Uncle Lar—'

'Oh, yes, indeed, posh through and through. I used to go hunting with hounds at the crack of dawn, Poppyducks. Eat pheasant and caviar for breakfast. Roast swans and piglets for lunch. And, in the evenings – guess where I went, Poppyducks?'

'To a banquet, Uncle Larry.'

'Top hole! The ladies – oh, the ladies wore mink and peacock feathers. The chaps boasted of shooting gazelles and tigers. And everyone picked their teeth with – can you guess, Poppyducks?'

'Platinum toothpicks decorated with precious gems, Uncle Larry.'

'Top-hole! But . . . oh, the posh, hoity-toity life bored me, Poppyducks. No imagination, you see. So I gave away my fortune – a donkey sanctuary in Paraguay being the main beneficiary – and with the money I got from selling the tiniest diamond from the shoddiest old toothpick: guess what I did, Poppyducks?'

'Bought this place, Uncle Larry. No. 5 Vinegar Street. And, while we're on the subject of buying houses, let me be the first to tell you the gobsmacking news about No. 7 –'

Something's coming!

Oh, what now? I was just about to tell –

No time! A van's approaching.

A van? What for?

Go and see.

'What about No. 7, Poppyducks?' asks Larry, pouring his shaken cocktail into a cocktail glass.

'Well . . . Mr Harmony was here earlier and –'

Go outside!

All right! All right!

'I've got to go, Uncle Larry. Sorry.'

'But, Poppyducks –'

'Farewell for now!'

— 3 —

A van is parked at the end of the street.

Across its side is written:

ELECTRICITY FOR A SPARKY LIFE

A man – wearing a very dark, buttoned-up uniform (must be uncomfortable in this heat, thinks Poppy) – gets out and consults a clipboard. Then looks round at the ruined houses and frowns in bewilderment.

'Greetings, Mr Electric Man.'

'What the –? Oh, you scared the living daylights out of me, you did.' He gives Poppy a double take. 'You going to a fancy-dress party?'

'Mercy me, no. Why say that?'

'Your outfit.'

'*I'm* not wearing an outfit, Mr Electricity Man.' Poppy clutches her handbag in front of her. 'It's *you* who's wearing an outfit. And, before you ask – yes, this is Vinegar Street. And – yes – that house is No. 7. My guess is you're here to turn the electric back on. Right?'

'What . . .? Oh, yeah.' Mr Electricity Man looks at No. 7. 'What a blooming dump.'

'That's a matter of opinion,' declares Poppy, indignantly. 'Personally, I've always thought it has the majesty of an ancient pyramid.'

Mr Electricity Man goes to the front door and fiddles with some keys.

That door's been locked all my born days, thinks Poppy. And now –

Wheeeeessshhhh!

Smell that! Oh, what a brew! Dead spiders! Mouldy mice! Rotting moths! Rat droppings! Dust! Can barely breathe –

And yet . . . look at Mr Electricity Man!

Going inside, calm as you please.

Can't he *smell* it? Can't he *feel* it? All those abandoned years gushing from the place!

Bzzz –

Wh . . . what's that?

Bzzzzz –

A vibration in the ground. Like millions of worms, burrowing at lightning speed and travelling towards –

No. 7!

It's the electric!

Of course! The house is sucking electricity like a newborn babe gasps air. But why can I feel it?

You're going to start *feeling lots of new things from now on!*

But . . . why should I feel new things?

— 13 —

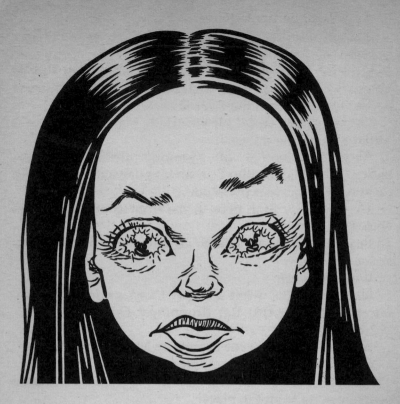

Buzzzz!
Oh, I don't like it!
There's a lot you won't like.
What? Tell me! Please –
Can't you guess?
The new neighbours?
Ten out of ten.
But why?
. . . Change.
Change? But . . . what will change?
Everything!
A flash!

An ancient lightbulb flares!

Bzzzzzzzzz –

Flash!

One by one, each room in the house flares like lightning.

The living room – Bzzz! Flash!

The bedroom – Bzzz! Flash!

Bathroom – Bzzz! Flash!

And each sixty-watt flare makes Poppy flinch as if she were part of the crackling current. She imagines the plug sockets sparkle with energy, eagerly awaiting the prospect of TVs, radios, computers, lamps, microwaves, fridges, cookers . . . Oh yes, the sockets are craving it now! Craving all the things that will turn No. 7 from a derelict shell into a –

Bzzz!

Flash!

– home!

Slowly, Poppy backs away . . .

Look at the place! she thinks. It looks . . .

Alive?

Precisely.

— **4** —

Poppy is sitting at the desk in her bedroom. She takes the objects from her handbag and spreads them in front of her. Illuminated by candlelight ('Nothing unlocks the creative juices like a flickering flame,' Poppy insists), they resemble the remains of a lost civilization.

Tin can!

Doll's arm –

I've got an old dustbin lid somewhere. Where is it . . .? Ah! Here! Now, if I stick this doll's arm to the edge! There! Now I've got some other dolls' arms just here. I found them in the ruins of No. 3 ages ago. Now . . . if I stick them round the edge of the dustbin lid as well –

Oh, it's difficult to concentrate when there's so much on my mind. Why is the tingling feeling tormenting me like this? It's never done it before –

'Can in come I – ooo, SweetiePops?'

'Mercy me, FudgeMa. You don't have to ask.'

'Disturb you didn't want to – ooo.'

Fudge shuffles into the room and perches on the edge of the mattress. She is small and thin with long, feathery hair. She's wearing a sari decorated with butterflies, sandals, and so many beads and bangles she jingles like sleigh bells. In one hand she's holding a very large, Japanese-style fan (a present from Uncle Larry) and in the other –

'Tea you for cup of ooo – SweetiePops.'

Now, as you've probably gathered, Fudge doesn't talk in the usual way. All the correct words are there, but not necessarily in the right order. So, for example, a sentence like, 'Cup of tea for you, SweetiePops,' comes out as . . . well, like you've just heard. Shorter sentences are not too difficult to understand. Longer ones, naturally, require a little more thought. Especially as Fudge intersperses most things with a worried, 'Ooooo'.

'Many thanks, FudgeMa,' says Poppy, taking a sip of tea. 'What do you think of my new Creation?'

'You do everything – oooo – can!'

'Oh, don't be silly, FudgeMa.'

But, to be honest, it certainly seems as if Poppy *can* do

everything. As well as the hundreds of little models made from rubbish (her Creations, as Poppy calls them), there are piles of drawings, paintings (including some quite sensitive watercolours of the Nuclear Power Plant), and exercise books full of stories, poems and ideas for novels.

'Something or bug – ooo!'

'What's that, FudgeMa? Oh, my new Creation! Yes, it does look like a bug or something. All those legs, eh? A centipede perhaps?'

'Oooo – no! Spider!'

'A spider! Yes!'

'Spider outer from – oooo – space.'

'A spider from outerspace! What a wonderful imagination you have, FudgeMa. In fact, that's *just* what I'm going to call it: SpaceSpider! How does that sound?'

'Love you – ooo!' Fudge gives Poppy a hug and a kiss, then stares thoughtfully into her daughter's eyes. 'Wrong what's, SweetiePops?'

Mercy me! FudgeMa can read me like a book. Of course something's wrong. I've got this tingling voice inside driving me doolally. *And* No. 7's been sold. And . . . well, all my life Vinegar Street has been me, FudgeMa, Auntie Bruiser and Uncle Larry. But now all that's going to change. And it sounds as if I'm not going to like it. But . . . oh, FudgeMa is looking forward to the new neighbours arriving and . . . well, I don't want to worry her for no reason –

There is a reason!

But what? Tell me specifics!

'Well, SweetiePops?'

'Oh . . . er . . . nothing, FudgeMa. I'm just a little tired.'

'You work hard too, SweetiePops! Have night an early! Don't want one of your headaches nasty – ooo, SweetiePops.'

'Precisely, FudgeMa. I don't want one of my nasty

headaches. I'll finish my cuppa and go straight to sleep. Sweet dreams, FudgeMa.'

'Dreams sweet, SweetiePops.'

Won't be dreams sweet for long.

— 5 —

'Beloved partners of Vinegar Street, we're gathered here today to say so long to Old Gal . . . Oh, I'm no good with words!'

'Say what you feel, Auntie Bruiser!'

'Speak from your muscular gut, Bruiserducks.'

'Feel what you say – ooo, SweetieBruiser.'

Earlier this morning, Bruiser had put the remains of Old Gal (reassembled, oiled and polished) into a grave she'd dug. Afterwards, she'd scrubbed an old paving-stone and (with more than a little help from Poppy) written on it:

**IN LOVING MEMORY
OF
OLD GAL
beloved motorbike of
Bruiser
and her best partners
Deputy Pops, Deputy Fudge and Deputy Larry
R. I. P.
(Rev In Peace)**

'Wobbling wagonwheels!' Bruiser fiddles nervously with her cowboy hat. 'Say what I feel! Speak from my gut! My heart! Well, all I'm thinking of is . . . the day I bought her.'

'Tell us about that, Auntie Bruiser.'

Bruiser takes a deep breath and, still looking unsure about the whole thing, continues, 'It was the day I was moving to my new homestead, as I recall. Yessiree! I'd staked my claim to a homestead in a brand new town called Vinegar Street! Out in the middle of nowhere it was. The nearest stagecoach – or bus, to you folks – stopped miles away. Now don't get me wrong, partners. I ain't complaining. The wilderness was just what I was yearning for. I'd had about a bellyful of people laughing at my cowboy hat and the way I talked and walked. Trouble was . . . well, strutting across that wilderness can be hazardous for a natural-born cowboy like myself. Poisonous snakes! Scorpions! Sun-stroke! You know what I needed?'

'A faithful stallion, Auntie Bruiser!'

'Bless your hide, yes! And that's when I saw Old Gal. Grazing in a stable – or parked in a garage, to you folks.' Bruiser's eyes glisten with the memory. 'How beautiful she was! All shining and groomed. And looking at me like we'd been friends for ever. I knew I had to have her. So . . . well, I tied my suitcases to her, then jumped on myself. What a weight it must have been. But did Old Gal buck or complain? No sirree. Just galloped off, brave as you please. Avoiding rattlesnakes and scorpions. Taking me all the way to my new homestead – No. 6 Vinegar Street!'

'And there was only one other person here, wasn't there, Auntie Bruiser?' cries Poppy, jumping up and down with excitement. 'FudgeMa! Although she wasn't strictly a Ma yet because she was still only pregnant with me –'

Something's coming!

Oh, not again! Please!

Take a look!

'What's wrong, DeputyPops?'

'What is it, Poppyducks?'

'What, SweetiePops?'

'Forgive me, everyone, what was I saying . . .?'

Take a look!

But –

You'll be sorry if you don't!

'Forgive me, everyone!' says Poppy, rushing to the street. 'But we should look outside.'

— 6 —

There it is!

A distant spot on the horizon – pulsating in the scorching summer heat – getting closer . . . closer . . .

'Looks like we've got visitors, partners!'

'Certainly looks a riff-raff vehicle.'

'Oooo – a it's lorry!'

'Of course, FudgeMa!' cries Poppy. 'To deliver the –'

Furniture!

I'd guessed that!

Took your time.

Shut up!

Temper, temper.

The lorry was gleaming and black, like a dead whale's hearse, and had pneumatic brakes that wheezed and gasped. Across the side was written:

MOVING MADE EAZIE

'Watchya, luvs 'n' guvs,' says a man, jumping out of the lorry.

'Greetings, Mr Lorry Driver.'

'Howdy, partner.'

'Delighted, my good man.'

'Afternoon good – ooo.'

Mr Lorry Driver opens the back of the lorry and calls, 'All right, mate?'

'Survivin',' replies another, poking his head out. Then, noticing the assembled throng, bellows, 'Watchya, luvs 'n' guvs!'

'Greetings, Mr Lorry Driver's Mate.'

'Howdy, partner.'

'Delighted, my good man.'

'Afternoon good – ooo.'

The two men huff 'n' puff in the back of the lorry for a while, then reappear holding a sofa between them.

'Got it, mate?'

'Got it, mate.'

They carry it up to No. 7's front door. Mr Lorry Driver takes some keys from his pocket and they go inside.

Noises can be heard as they place the sofa in the living room.

'Here, mate!'

'Sure, mate?'

'Positive, mate!'

'Right, mate!'

The two men come out, mopping their brows.

'Who . . . who's moving in?' asks Poppy.

'Can't tell you that, luv.'

'Mercy me, why?'

'Rules is rules, luv.'

They don't know, do they?

N☺.

Don't *you* know?

I do. You don't.
Just tell me! Please!
Look at the furniture.
But I want to know –
Look!
An armchair!
A cooker!
Curtains!
'Stampeding stallions! I've never seen so many frills

and lacey bits.'

'Floral patterns! Lots of pink! Perfectly riff-raff!'

'Everything's – ooo – clean so!'

Oh . . . what's that feeling?

It's the furniture.

What do you mean?

Every object has soaked up the emotions of its owners. And now those emotions are seeping out –

Into me.

You bet.

But . . . oh, I don't like it. There's so many bad feelings. There's discontent in the frying pan. Disappointment in the microwave. Oh, make it stop! Please! Make it stop!

I'm not doing it. You are.

But it's never happened before –

Cabinet*Sorrow*!

*Anger*Dressing table!

Tupperware*Heartache*!

My head's beginning to throb! Oh, no! I'm getting one of my headaches! Blobs appearing in front of my eyes! Pain –

*Loss*Alarm clock *Upset*Radio *Spite*Bookcase *Bossiness* –

Headache . . . getting worse! Filling my mind –

*PRESSURE*RUBBERPLANT*TORMENT*BLANKET-*PAIN*FRAMEDPHOTOGRAPH*OPPRESSIVENESS*-CHINADOLL*STRAIN* –

— 7 —

– *AGITATION* TELEPHONE*JITTERINESS* CHANDELIER *MISERY* –
'. . . alm down, DeputyPo . . .'
'. . . lax, Poppyduc . . .'
'. . . wind, Sweetie . . .'
JUG*PLEASURE* MAGAZINES *CALMNESS* –
'Calm down, DeputyPops.'
'Relax, Poppyducks.'
'Unwind, Sweetiepops.'
Pillowcase *Contentment* Candlesticks –
'Calm down, Deputy – Look! She's coming round!'
'Hear me, Poppyducks?'
'Me hear – ooo, SweetiePops?'
The headache's nearly gone now! Where am I? I'm in my room! On my bed! And – look! Auntie Bruiser is rubbing my temples! Uncle Larry is massaging my feet! And FudgeMa is fanning me. They always do this when I get one of my headaches. And it always does the trick because . . . yes, it's –

. . .

– gone!
'You can stop rubbing now, Auntie Bruiser. You can stop massaging now, Uncle Larry. And FudgeMa, rest your wrist, I pray. Another success for the Vinegar Street Emergency Headache Treatment!'
'Suffering cactus!' declares Bruiser. 'These darned

headaches of yours have just got to stop.'

'I don't *want* to get them, Auntie Bruiser –'

'Well, spit in my stetson, I know that, DeputyPops. It's just that darned mind of yours. It's over . . . over – oh, what's the word?'

'Cooked – ooo – over!'

'Overcooked is right, DeputyFudge! All this . . .' She looks round the bedroom. 'Your Creations! Your drawings! Your writing –'

'But I *have* to do them, Auntie Bruiser!'

'Wobbling wagonwheels, I know that too! And mighty proud of you we all are. Why, you've got more talent in your left nostril than all our noses put together. But, sometimes, you've just got to . . . well, give that brain a rest, DeputyPops. Why, only last week, you got overcooked because you were trying to work out how many doorknobs to stick on one of your Creations.'

'It wasn't *how many*, Auntie Bruiser. It was *what colour*! And what an important decision! Blue, I decided. But then another problem. What *type* of blue. There're so many: navy blue, cobalt blue, hyacinth blue, duck-egg blue, Oxford blue, peacock blue, sapphire blue, pthalo blue, ultramarine blue –'

'Woah, DeputyPops, woah! There you go again! Galloping off like a herd of spooked cattle.'

'Mercy me! I'm . . . I'm sorry! I do take these things very seriously. And I *will* try not to . . . *overcook* myself in future. But, to be honest, today's headache wasn't caused by anything to do with . . . with my Creations.'

'Know I what,' says FudgeMa, stroking Poppy's hair. 'It's – oooo – the neighbours new.'

'No secrets from you, FudgeMa. And, yes, it *is* the new neighbours – Oh, don't look at me like that. I know you're going to think I'm being silly but . . . oh, I can't help it. You see, all my life it's just been us. But now . . . there's going to be new neighbours. And I have this . . . this feeling. Oh, don't ask me to explain it. But . . . I'm afraid things are going to change. And I don't want them to.' And, suddenly, huge tears brim in Poppy's eyes. 'I don't want to change, FudgeMa!' she sobs. 'Please! Don't let it happen!'

FudgeMa takes Poppy in her arms and rocks her gently. 'Never, SweetiePops – ooo! Hush now, hush! Us always! Always love! Change that nothing can! Us love always for ever!'

'Darned right!' declares Auntie Bruiser, holding Poppy. 'Us love always for ever!'

'Indubitably, yes,' Uncle Larry agrees, holding Poppy. 'Us love always for ever.'

'Us love always for ever!' cries Poppy, holding them all. 'Oh, yes! Precisely! Us love always for ever. US LOVE ALWAYS FOR EVER!'

Feel better now?

Yes.

Won't last.

— 8 —

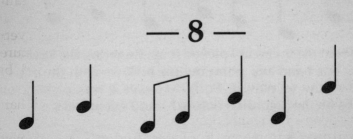

That feeling. Just a few notes on GusPa's accordion and I feel . . . oh, like I'm being protected by the strongest arms in the whole world –

Won't last.

Stop saying that –

'I'm to bed going, SweetiePops.'

'Oh . . . you getting an early night, FudgeMa?'

'Tired very – ooo – yes. But keep playing on.'

'You sure, FudgeMa? Don't want to . . . upset you.'

'No, no, no, SweetiePops. Good hear to you play – ooo, yes. Reminds of me your GusPa. How proud you of would he have been . . . how proud, how proud.'

'Sweet dreams, FudgeMa.'

'Dreams sweet, SweetiePops.'

Poor FudgeMa. She still misses GusPa so much. Every time she talks about him her eyes get watery. Oh . . . how I wish I'd known GusPa. He died before I was born. FudgeMa loved him very much. Love at first sight, she says. I asked her once what being in love was like. She said her blood tingled and fizzed like it was full of sherbet. A fever of sherbet. Oh, how glorious! Wish I'd known GusPa. All I've got left of him are his security pass (he worked at the Nuclear Power Plant), that big alarm clock beside my bed, and this . . . this glorious accordion –

From the moment I picked it up, fingering the keyboard with one hand and pumping the bellows with the other, I knew how to play it. FudgeMa says I was picking out tunes on the accordion before I could even speak –

Oh, what bliss! Sitting at my desk. Candlelight flickering across my SpaceSpider. Window open . . . Sound of insects . . . Gentle breeze . . . Music . . .

It's so dark outside. Clouds must be covering the moon. But I don't need to see the street . . . I can *feel* it. My world. Next door, the rubble of No. 2. Then next to that, the ruins of No. 3. Then, cross the street, and coming back down the other side, the remains of No. 4, then No. 5 (where Uncle Larry lives), No. 6 (where Auntie Bruiser lives) and, finally, No. 7, the house directly opposite –

Something –

Leave me alone!

Not my fault. It's starting.

What?

Look out of the window.

All right! I'm looking . . .

Oh, it's so dark. Auntie Bruiser and Uncle Larry must be having an early night too –

You see it?

Where?

There! In the distance.

Headlights!

What a genius!

Getting closer.

What a genius!

You've already said that. If you're going to make wisecracks, please be original . . . Is it a car coming?

Not saying.

Don't sulk.

. . . It's a taxi.

Who's in it?

Can't you guess?

New neighbour?

Big danger.

— 9 —

Poppy blows her candles out.

A taxi pulls into Vinegar Street.

It comes to a halt outside No. 7.

But . . . oh, the angle it's stopped at! The headlights are shining right in my eyes. Can't see anything! Not a thing –

'That'll be ten quid, luv,' Mr Taxi Driver says.

The clinking of coins.

'Keep the change!' says a woman's voice.

So it's a woman! thinks Poppy.

Yes. It's a woman.

Then –

Footsteps.

Jangling of keys.

Key in lock.

Oh, I wish the taxi would go! I want to see what this new neighbour looks like. Why doesn't the TingleVoice tell me some more?

TingleVoice! I've got a name at last. And I like it too! Look – she's unlocking the front door.

I can't! The headlights are hurting my eyes –

Front door unlocking.

Taxi starts moving away –

Creak of front door opening.

Taxi drives off!

Light out of my eyes!

Just in time to see –
Front door closing!
I've missed her!
Look closer!
She's . . . she's glancing out from behind the half-open door. Oh . . . her eyes! They're blazing! Like two red lights. Monster's eyes!
The door shuts!
Silence . . .
Danger has found a home!
You're scaring me!
Good!

— PART TWO —

HumCrazy

— 10 —

'. . . la-de-dah . . . la-de-dah . . .'

Poppy's eyes click open.

'. . . la-de-dum . . .'

What *is* that, TingleVoice?

The new neighbour.

Poppy rushes to the window!

She's in there! And she's . . . oh, just listen to that humming. I've never heard a more irritating sound. Oh, TingleVoice, why don't you just explain everything now? Stop playing games with me. What danger? What changes? Specify? Please.

Where's the fun in that?

And what if you're wrong?

Have I ever been wrong before?

There's always a first time, TingleVoice.

Never. Just *look* at her house. All the curtains are up already. And they've been pulled shut. Every window. Why? What's she hiding?

Hiding?

Think about it — Aha! Your FudgeMa's just got up.

Well, there you *must* be wrong. It's only two minutes past six o'clock. FudgeMa never gets up this early.

Ready for this? Three, two, one —

'What sound that is – oooo, SweetiePops?'

'Oh . . . FudgeMa . . . you *are* up.'

'Humming me woke, SweetiePops.'

Told you so.

All right, all right.

'It's . . . it's the new neighbour, FudgeMa. She arrived last night. Under cover of darkness. Just like a spy!'

'Don't silly be!' FudgeMa rubs her bleary eyes, then looks at the house opposite. 'She happy sounds!'

'She *lunatic* sounds! Listen to it! She must suffer from diarrhoea of the vocal chords or something. And why's she got the curtains pulled, FudgeMa? Ask yourself that! Every window! What's she doing in there – apart from her half-witted humming – that she's so ashamed of? What's she hiding?'

That's the spirit.

You're giving me a headache.

Take an aspirin.

'Morning, partners!' hollers Bruiser, closing her front door.

'That demented caterwauling wake you too, Auntie Bruiser?'

Bruiser strides down the street, her many buckled boots chink-chinking. 'Can't say it did, DeputyPops! I've got myself a spot of shopping to do! And it's a long trek across that wilderness now Old Gal's gone.' She comes to a chinking halt beneath their window. 'Anything I can get you folks while I'm at the store?'

Ask for a new exercise book.

But I don't need –

You will.

But –

I'm never wrong!

'I'm in dire need of a new exercise book, Auntie Bruiser.'

'No problem, DeputyPops. So long, partners.'

'Bye – ooo – Bruiser.'

'Farewell, Auntie Bruis– Oh, FudgeMa, that humming! It's driving me crazy!'

— 11 —

'. . . and then FudgeMa cooked some kippers for breakfast. I put extra butter on mine. Comfort food, it's called. And, mercy me, did I need comforting! That humming went on and on . . . You listening, Uncle Larry?'

'Wh . . . what, Poppyducks?'

'I'm delivering the most important news in the history of Vinegar Street and all you're doing is twitching and scratching.'

'Oh, do forgive me, Poppyducks!' sighs Uncle Larry, stretching out on the sofa and twitching and scratching even more. 'It's just that . . . well, I had a few cocktails last night. And now I've got one of those frightfully fidgety hangovers. My whole body feels full of cockroaches wearing spikey stilettoes. And it makes listening to your news – important though it undoubtedly is – frightfully tricky.' Twitch, twitch. 'Do you think you could . . .?' And he gazes longingly at the cocktail cabinet.

'A cocktail!' gasps Poppy. 'But it's not even midday yet!'

'I know, I know, Poppyducks! I'm a disgraceful human being. But it's the only cure for the stilettoed cockroaches! I'm afraid I might drop one of the bottles if I' – twitch,

scratch – 'Oh, I'd be greatly obliged, Poppyducks.'

'You really must stop all those late-night cocktails!'
Poppy goes to the cocktail bar and asks, 'Which bottle
first?'

'The green one, Poppyducks.'

Poppy puts a dash from the green bottle in the cocktail
shaker. 'Next?'

'The pink bottle, and please, Poppyducks, pray
continue with your important news – and that's four
dashes of pink by the way, Poppyducks.'

'One! So, after breakfast I help FudgeMa wash up –
Two! – and I'm just about to go to my room to start work
on SpaceSpider – Three! – when FudgeMa looks at the
clock and says, "Should enough by now time – oooo!"
And I know exactly what she means! She's going to go

over to No. 7 to say, "Welcome". Which bottle next, Uncle Larry?'

'The orange one. Three dashes, if you please.'

'So,' continues Poppy, 'FudgeMa asks me if I want to go with her – One! – and half of me does and half of me doesn't. I'm curious to see the new neighbour, yes! What kind of person can just hum and hum like that? And yet, the other half is . . . well, let's just say wary – Two! – So, in the end, FudgeMa goes alone. I watch from behind the living-room curtains – Three! – FudgeMa goes up to No. 7 and knocks –'

'The blue!'

'Wh . . . what?'

'The next bottle! Blue!'

'Oh, mercy me, yes! Anyway, FudgeMa waits but no one answers –'

'No, no! The *blue* bottle!'

'This *is* the blue bottle.'

'No, it's not! Or rather – oh, I suppose it *is* a blue. But I mean the other blue bottle, Poppyducks.'

'There is no *other* blue bottle.'

'There is! There! At the end!'

'That's *purple*, Uncle Larry. You see? A touch of red in the colour –'

'Five dashes from the purple bottle then! Please hurry, Poppyducks!'

'I'd be a lot faster if you were precise about your colours. One! – So FudgeMa knocks again. A little louder this time – Two! – The humming stops inside the house – Three! – FudgeMa waits – Four! – But does the new neighbour open the door? No! She just starts humming again. Ignoring FudgeMa – Five! – What next?'

'Put the lid on the cocktail shaker!'

'And shake?'

'Most vigorously, Poppyducks!'

'What a rude woman!' Shake-shake! 'Don't you think, Uncle Larry?' Shake-shake-shake! 'To ignore FudgeMa like that!'

'Enough shaking, Poppyducks. Don't bother with a glass. I'll drink it just as it is . . . Thanks awfully!'

Mercy me! I've never seen him gulp a cocktail so fast! And what a noise! Like dirty dishwater going down a plug-hole.

'Feeling better, Uncle Larry?'

'Top hole, Poppyducks.'

'Uncle Larry, has it occurred to you that you might be developing a problem with your drink –'

Something's coming!

Wh . . . what now?

Mr Harmony!

'Excuse me, Uncle Larry, but I've just got to dash outside. And be careful. You're dribbling cocktail all over your dressing gown.'

— 12 —

See it?

Yes, TingleVoice.

A spot quivering in the scorching heat.

I don't see Mr Harmony for one year, two months and six days and now it's almost a daily event –

Clunk!

Clunk!

Ka-chung.

'Greetings, Mr Harmony.' Poppy strides over. 'What brings you to our wonderful abode today?'

'Stop that sarcasm right now,' pants Mr Harmony, struggling to get out of the car. 'Guess what state my nerves are in?' He dabs a sweaty handkerchief over his sunburnt head. 'A *shocking* state, that's what. A million electric eels changing a light bulb in the middle of an electrical storm are living a life of shock-free tranquillity compared to me. Now, if you'll excuse me . . .' He takes several sheets of paper from his jacket pocket. 'I've got some documents need signing.'

'By the new neighbour?'

'Who else?'

'You'll be lucky.'

'Oh, don't tell me she's gone out. I told her I'd be here today at–'

'Oh, she's in all right. Just not opening the door. FudgeMa knocked and knocked and was totally ignored for her pains! And look at those curtains. Still pulled. And the day's half gone. Honestly, Mr Harmony, what kind of people are you letting live in your houses these days?'

He's never met her!

But . . . he must have.

It was all done by letter and phone!

'Well, she might not open her door to any of you,' says Mr Harmony, flicking sweat from his eyes, 'but, then again, who can blame her? You're all weirdos.'

'Many thanks, Mr Harmony.'

'It's not meant to be a compliment! I'm trying to insult you.'

'Then you'll just have to try harder, Mr Harmony. And, by the way, a word of advice: you really should wear a hat in this weather. You'll get sunstroke with your bald head.'

'I'm *not* bald.'

'You're . . . not?'

'No! I've got very *fine* hair, that's all.'

'Well, yes, I'm sure they're very fine hairs. All thirty-five of them.'

'Why don't you give that sarcastic tongue of yours a rest,' growls Mr Harmony, 'and let me get on with my job.' And, with that, Mr Harmony marches up to No. 7 and –

Knock! Knock!

'It's Mr Harmony!'

And then –

The door opens a little.

'Good morning, Mrs Nylon,' says Mr Harmony.

And then . . .

Mr Harmony is let inside the house.

Thunk!

The door closes behind him.

'Mrs Nylon,' ponders Poppy. 'So her name's Mrs Nylon!'

Otherwise known as —

The Biggest Danger! I get the point!

— 13 —

'They've been in there for five hours and twenty-two minutes now!' says Poppy, peeking through the living-room curtains at the house opposite. 'What can they be doing?'

'Relax, Poppyducks.'

'Unwind – ooo, SweetiePops!'

'But I *can't* relax, Uncle Larry. I can't unwind, FudgeMa! Not when there's always something new to tense and wind me. The endless humming! The curtains kept pulled! Ignoring us when we knock . . .! Hear that? The sound of Mrs Nylon giggling! Like a hyena being strangled!' Poppy presses her nose against the window-pane. 'Show yourself, Mrs Nylon! I want to see what you look like!'

'Perhaps she privacy wants – ooo, SweetiePops.'

'Privacy! On Vinegar Street? Don't make me laugh!'

'Well, all I can say is I heard her humming earlier and it sounded frightfully . . . pleasant.'

'Pleasant!' gasps Poppy, staring at Uncle Larry. 'I'd rather listen to an elephant fart!'

'Poppyducks!'

'SweetiePops!'

'Well, I'm sorry, but I seem to be the only one who finds it the most irritating racket in the cosmos. Look at you both! Slouched on the sofa, dunking biscuits into cups of tea, as if you haven't a care in the world.'

'But I haven't, Poppyducks.'

'You *have*, Uncle Larry! We *all* have! That humming and giggling lunatic opposite! She's a danger – Oh, there! I've said it now! But . . . well, she is! I'm sure of it. A danger. Don't ask me how I know. I just . . . just feel it.'

'What sort of danger, Poppyducks?'

'Yes – ooo, SweetiePops?'

'I . . . I'm not sure yet – Oh, careful, Uncle Larry, soggy biscuit has dropped all down your dressing gown. Honestly! If you don't show your clothes the inside of a washing machine pretty soon, they'll jump from the top of a building in suicidal despair.'

Something's happening!

You bet! You've made my nerves so bad, I've blurted out all this danger stuff before I was ready –

Go outside.
I'm fed up with you bossing me –
It's Auntie Bruiser! Go outside! Now!
'Everyone! Follow me!'
'What – ooo – Sweetie –?'
'What is it, Poppy –?'
'COME ON!'

— 14 —

VROOOOM!!!
A motorbike speeds into the street.
Dust billows behind.
Paintwork sparkles.
Chrome glints.
Auntie Bruiser's holding the handlebars with one hand while, in the other, she waves her cowboy hat, as if riding a bucking bronco –
'YEEEE-HAAAA!!'
Up and down the street she goes.
At each end, she does a wheelie.
The engine roars like a wild animal.
'Glorious, Auntie Bruiser!'
'Top hole, Bruiserducks!'
'Wonderful – ooo, SweetieBruiser!'
'Thanking you kindly, partners!' she bellows, screeching the bike to a halt in front of them. 'Weren't expecting another stallion in town so soon, eh? But . . .

well, after Old Gal's funeral and DeputyPops' headache, I reckoned we needed something to put the smile back on our darned faces! Say a neighbourly howdy to New Gal.'

'New Gal!' gasps Poppy. 'What a glorious name, Auntie Bruis–'

He's coming out!

Mr Harmony?

Who else? Look! The door to No. 7's opening and—

'Tatty-bye, Mrs Nylon!' coos Mr Harmony, closing the door and skipping towards his car.

'Howdy, Mr Harmony,' says Auntie Bruiser.

'Good day, my dear Mr Harmony,' says Uncle Larry.

'Day good – ooo, Mr Harmony.'

'Stop that sarcasm, you lot,' snaps Mr Harmony. 'I built these homes in good faith! Hear me? I hired the best carpenters, the most experienced electricians, and the trustworthiest bricklayers! It's not my fault the street ended up like this. You know who I blame? *You* lot!'

'*Us*, Mr Harmony!' gasps Poppy.

'You bet your sweet patootie, Little Miss Sarcastic. None of you take care of anything. Just look at the state of you. A shaven-headed woman with more muscles than a hyperactive lumberjack! A grown man, wearing a dressing gown in the middle of the afternoon – with soggy biscuit all down the front! A lanky, straggly-haired girl, dressed like something from a horror film –'

'Many thanks, Mr Harmony!'

'It's not a compliment!' yells Mr Harmony, stamping his foot. Then he clutches his chest and continues, 'Oh, my heart! I'm a sick man! I'm as frazzled as a hundred rashers of bacon in a frying pan being cooked at midday in the middle of the Sahara Desert.' He struggles into his car. 'I was in such a good mood talking to Mrs Nylon. She understands me. She agrees with me. Oh, what a

woman!' His eyes glimmer with admiration as he repeats
slowly, 'What a woman . . . What a woman . . . What a
woman . . .'

'Suffering cactus,' sighs Bruiser, watching him drive off.
'That man never changes!'

She's wrong.

How do you mean?

Mr Harmony has changed.

In what way?

Couldn't you tell?

No.

Think about it! The way he skipped over
to his car. How talking to Mrs Nylon put him
in such a good mood. The way he repeated,
'What a woman' over and over again.

You mean . . .?

Mmm?

Our Mr Harmony is . . . is . . .?

Go on.

With Mrs Nylon?

Top marks!

'Mr Harmony's in love!' blurts Poppy.

— 15 —

'In love!' gasps Bruiser.

'In love!' gasps Larry.

'In love!' gasps Fudge.

'Oh . . . I'm sorry, everyone. I didn't mean to blurt it out like that. But – yes! I'm sure of it. And with that Mrs Nylon too. Didn't you see the way he was skipping and – oh, it's obvious! And, if that's the case, the situation's just gone from bad to worse!'

'But why should it, DeputyPops?'

'Yes, why, Poppyducks?'

'Yes, why – ooo – SweetiePops?'

'Because he'll be on *her* side. And she's dangerous.'

That's the spirit!

Oh, I've had enough! I want to see this woman –

'COME OUT! SHOW YOURSELF!' yells Poppy.

Bravo! Bravo!

'DeputyPops!'

'Poppyducks!'

'SweetiePops!'

'COME OUT! WHAT ARE YOU ASHAMED OF?'

'Wobbling wagonwheels, DeputyPops! Calm down! You really are making a stampede out of a gallop!'

'I can't calm down, Auntie Bruiser. I have to see her – THIS IS POPPY PICKLESTICKS OF NO. 1 VINEGAR STREET! YOUR FELLOW NEIGHBOURS ARE ALL HERE! WE WANT TO SAY HELLO AND WELCOME YOU TO OUR STREET. COME OUT, MRS NYLON! COME OUT! COME OUT!'

Oh, such authority!

She can't ignore me! Not after that! What do you think, TingleVoice?

I think she's going to start humming again in a moment as if nothing's happened.

But . . . oh, she wouldn't dare!

Get ready. Three, two, one –

'. . . la-de-da . . .'

'Listen to that!' Poppy cries. 'The rudeness of the woman! The rudeness! I'm going to knock on her door.'

That's my girl!

'Where are you going, DeputyPops?'

'What are you doing, Poppyducks?'

'What – ooo, where, SweetiePops?'

'TO KNOCK!' shrieks Poppy, spinning to face them and stamping her foot. 'AND I'M GOING TO KEEP ON KNOCKING AND KNOCKING UNTIL THAT . . . THAT IGNORANT HUMMING MONSTROSITY OPENS THE – What's wrong? Why . . . why you all looking at me like that?'

They're not looking at you.

What . . . what do you mean?

They're looking behind you.

Behind? Oh, don't tell me! While I was ranting and raving Mrs Nylon opened her door and –

She's going to speak. Get ready. Three, two, one —

'Peek-a-boo, everyone!'

— 16 —

I want to turn round. But I can't.

Scared?

No. Just embarrassed.

She's coming up behind you —

'What *mussst* you think of me? Hiding mysssself away like that. What a rude new neighbour, you mussst have thought. But there was jusssst *ssso* much to do. All that housssework! Will you forgive me? Will you? Will you?'

'Mmm,' says Bruiser.

'Mmm,' says Larry.

'Oooo,' says Fudge.

Look at them! Speechless! Eyes agog! This Mandy Nylon must look quite horrific – Oh, what's that?

Her breath on your neck.

Ugh!

Move then!

I can't! I'm frozen!

'Thank you ssso very much! Without your forgivenesss, I'd have been ssso heartbroken! Really I would! Oh, it's ssso fantassstic to meet you all. Really! You mussst be Misss Bruiser?'

'At your service, ma'am.'

'Oh, how thrilling! And what a firm handshake! You're

a natural-born pioneer, if ever I sssaw one, Miss Bruiser.'

Listen to her! If she crawls any lower she'll be on her way to Australia.

Your Auntie Bruiser is lapping it up.

'And you mussst be Mr Larry?'

'Charmed, my dear madam!'

'Oh, be ssstill my heart. I've never been kisssed on the hand before. What charm! What . . . *breeding*! That'sss the word! Noble blood is sssomething one is born with and you've obviousssly got the full eight pintsss, Mr Larry.'

I'm going to puke! That voice! It's as fake as they come. And those hissing 's's are setting my teeth on edge.

Your Uncle Larry doesn't seem to be bothered.

No. Look at him. Lapping it up too.

'And you mussst be Miss Fudge!'

'Oooooo – do you how do?'

'Well, I'm all the better for meeting you, Miss Fudge. And what beautiful hands you have! Look at them! Sssmall, delicate, and with sssuch sssoft ssskin. You mussst give me tipsss on how you keep them ssso young, Miss Fudge.'

FudgeMa too! Lapping it up! What's wrong with everyone? How can they be fooled by that sickening voice? It's like the sweetest candyfloss with a zillion cherries on top –

'Thisss mussst be your daughter, Miss Fudge. Oh, she is *ssso* cute! What'sss her name?'

'ASK ME!' yells Poppy, spinning round to face her. 'I'VE GOT A BLOOMING TONGUE!'

That's telling her, kid.

Don't call me kid.

'DeputyPops!'

'Poppyducks!'

'SweetiePops!'

'Oh, don't be ssso hard on her,' says Mandy Nylon in her frothiest voice. 'Mussst be the heat! Putsss usss all in a ratty mood sssometimes. Now, tell me your name, you cute little girl.'

Tell her then!

I . . . I can't speak.

Why?

Well . . . just look at her! She's not horrific at all. She's . . . she's . . .

What?

She's . . . glamour!

— 17 —

Mandy Nylon's not very tall. About the same size as Fudge. But, in every other respect, she couldn't be more different:look at her hair! So long! So blond! Bursting with waves and curls! And her face . . . have you ever seen such perfect make-up? Frosty-pink lipstick (on pouting lips), surrounding neon-white teeth (her dentist must be a very rich person), mascara and eyeshadow (around large, crystal-clear eyes). And look at what she's wearing! Or, rather, what she's *not* wearing! For her dress is cut so low, so short and so tight that every bulge and curve (of her ever-so bulging and curvaceous body) yells, 'Hello! I'm here!' The outfit is completed by the highest stilettos you've ever seen (How does she walk on them? thinks Poppy) and nails so long and varnished it's a wonder she can pick anything up.

'My name . . . is Poppy,' Poppy manages.

'Poppy!' breathes Mandy. '*Ssso* cute! Oh, pleassse, Poppy, don't be angry with me. I know it was rude not to talk mature woman to cute little girl. But . . . well, you did have your back to me. Didn't you? Didn't you?'

'Well . . . yes.'

'Ssso who was rude firssst? Me or you?'

'Well . . . me, I suppose.'

'What a clever little girl! And jussst *ssso* cuuute! At least' – and here she peers closer at Poppy – 'you have the *posssibility* of cutenesss.'

'The . . . possibility?'

'Why, of courssse. Jussst look at your eyes, for example. Ssso big. But you're not making the mossst of them.'

'I'm . . . not?'

'Not at all. You need a touch of massscara.'

'Mascara!'

'To bring out your lashesss. And sssome eyeshadow here.' Her long, varnished nails glint in front of Poppy's face like claws. 'And as for that dresss . . .'

'What's wrong with my dress?'

'What's *wrong*? Little girl, what'sss *right*? It does nothing for you. A girl should be brimful with ssswirls and curlsss. Not ssstraight as a lamp post.'

I'm gonna thump her!

Temper, temper.

'Look at me, for example,' continues Mandy Nylon, running her hands up and down her swirling and curving body. 'Not a ssstraight line in sssight. I'm total woman.'

Total crackpot more like!

'Anyway, mussstn't ssstand here chatting all day,' says Mandy Nylon, flashing everyone her widest smile. 'Much as I'd like to, that is. You're all sssuch a wonderful audience – I mean, company. I'm just ssso very glad we broke the ice. We're all going to be the bessst of friends in the whole wide world. Sssee you sssoon.'

— 18 —

Poppy pushes the plate of vindaloo away from her. 'I feel sick!' she grumbles, slumping back in her chair.

'DeputyPops!'

'Poppyducks!'

'SweetiePops! What's wrong? I thought loved vindaloo you – ooo?'

'I *do* love vindaloo, FudgeMa. And I love it when we're all together like this – at our kitchen table – munching and chattering. But *not* when the only topic of conversation seems to be Mandy Nylon! What nice hair Mandy has! What a good figure Mandy has! How pretty Mandy is.'

'Suffering cactus, DeputyPops, she *is* darned pretty. There's no denying that! Don't think I've ever seen such a well-formed filly.'

'With such spiffing hair.'

'Lovely nails – ooo – too.'

'Listen to yourselves! I feel like I've just landed on a planet called Act Like A Total Twerp. Shall I tell you what I see when I look at her? Big hair, big teeth and big boobs. That's all. And as for what she was wearing – well, it wasn't a dress, that's for sure. More like an *un*dress. Bursting out of it she was. Like someone poured her into it and forgot to say "when"! And all that "a girl should be brimful with swirls and curls" nonsense. I ask you! Bonkersville or what?'

'You're overreacting, DeputyPops.'

'I'm not *over*reacting. You're all *under*reacting. That woman . . . she told me to wear mascara. And change my clothes. Nothing like that has *ever* happened on Vinegar Street. Here – why, here we all wear exactly what we want. We . . . we *enjoy* each other's uniqueness. We *celebrate* it! But that woman . . . oh, that woman . . .! I bet she won't celebrate anything unless it looks . . . well, exactly like her!'

She's the Biggest Danger!

But how can I convince *them*? They're fully fledged members of the Mandy Nylon Fan Club. It wouldn't surprise me if FudgeMa doesn't run them up a few 'WE LOVE MANDY NYLON' T-shirts on her sewing machine.

You've got to get proof.

How . . . how do you mean?

Watch Mandy Nylon. Night and day.

And?

Before long . . . you'll see something.

Something to prove what a danger she is?

Exactly.

'Oh, listen . . . Listen, everyone! I'll show you I'm right. From tomorrow morning I'm going to get up at the crack of dawn and . . . and watch her. And I'll write down everything she does in that new exercise book you bought me, Auntie Bruiser.'

Told you you'd need it.

'But, honestly, Poppyducks, there's no need –'

'There's *every* need, Uncle Larry,' snaps Poppy, glaring in the direction of No. 7. 'That woman is a danger and I'm going to prove it. Besides . . . no one calls me cute and gets away with it!'

— 19 —

That night, Poppy has a dream.

She's wearing a nightdress and standing in a moonlit Vinegar Street.

This must be the most beautiful place in the whole world, she thinks. Look – the weeds resemble tropical plants from some unexplored jungle. Listen – insects droning, spiders spinning webs and beetles scurrying over broken glass. And smell – oh, at night the street has an exotic aroma all of its own –

BFFUM – FWOOOM.

A rhythmic rumble in the ground.

Like the footsteps of an approaching giant –

No! Not approaching!

It's here already!

In the street!

BFFUM – FWOOM!

BFFUMM – FWOOOM!

And getting louder too. Stronger. More regular!

Beating with the regularity of –

'A heartbeat!' cries Poppy.

A heartbeat coming from –

No. 7!

And then –

Bzzzz – Light!

Bzzzz – Light!

Two upstairs windows light up with the brilliance of

searchlights. And they glare down at Poppy like . . . dazzling eyes.

And then –

Creeeeak!

The front door swings open. And sucks in air. Like a . . . a mouth!

'Help!' cries Poppy. 'Heeellppp!'

But her cries are drowned by a new sound.

For now the house is speaking:

'THISSS SSSTREET IS MINE!!!'

— PART THREE —

Nylon Watch

— 20 —

7.00 – Humming heard

Mercy me! I didn't hear an alarm clock. She must wake up naturally. Lucky her! GusPa's alarm clock nearly gave me a heart attack this morning. Crack of dawn it clanged like a fire engine. Been sitting at my desk ever since. Like a spy in a watch tower! Notebook, pen, clock, binoculars – everything spread out in front of me. Of course, what I really need is an infra-red camera and a few microphones to bug her place –

Wait! What's she doing now? At last! Something happening! The front door is . . . yes! It's opening. There she is. Mercy me! She's got all her make-up on and her hair done! And she's wearing a tracksuit. And now she's–

7.30 – Jogging

Or, rather, she's *trying* to! Look at her! Dodging between all the rubble and weeds – Ooops! She's tripped! Can't help smiling. This woman really brings out the nasty side of me –

'Morning good – ooo, SweetiePops!'

'Greetings, FudgeMa. You're up early again. Was it the sound of the demented jogger from No. 7?'

'Really not, SweetiePops,' FudgeMa squeezes next to Poppy and looks out of the window. 'Your alarm clock me

woke – Oh, at Mandy look! What energy has she!'

'It's the energy of a lunatic! Don't wave, FudgeMa! I want to watch in secret. Like a scientist watches an animal in a laboratory. I'm studying all her nasty little habits –'

'What little habits nasty?'

'Well, jogging for one! I've never seen anything so revolting! Why can't she laze around all morning, eating kippers like the rest of us –?'

Something coming!

Oh, there you are, TingleVoice. Wondered where you'd gone. Had a lie-in this morning, did you?

Park your *lips* and *look* out of the window.

Who's coming, then?

Mr Harmony.

Again! Mercy, mercy!

Poppy cranes her head out of the window and – yes! There is a car coming. But –

That's not Mr Harmony.

Oh, ye of little faith.

But it's not his car.

Is!

Not! This car's all new and shiny. It's hardly making a sound as it parks outside No. 7 . . . It can't be Mr Harmony.

Keep watching.

Someone's getting out of the car. He's wearing a new suit. Not a crease. Except the ones in his trousers – sharp enough to slice cucumber. And the white shirt. And the . . . the . . .

Toupee!

'A wig!' gasps Poppy out loud. 'It *is* Mr Harmony and . . . he's wearing a wig. Blond with neat side-parting! How disgusting!'

Told you it was him.

And look! Mandy Nylon's seen him. She's running up to him and –

'Peek-a-boo, Mr Harmony! I jussst love your makeover!
Jussst love it, love it, love it! So dasssshing! So handsssome!
Didn't I tell you it would sssuit you? I'm the Queen of
Makeovers, me! What a business tycoon you look! Be
ssstill my beating heart! Look at my chessst rising and
falling in excitement. Come inssside and ssspend sssome
quality time with me, Mr Harmony.' She grabs hold of his
arm and squeals with delight. 'Oh, how handsssome your
hair is. I want to run my fingers through it.'

'Well, if he takes it off you can blow your nose on it too,'
mutters Poppy. Then, noticing FudgeMa's look, adds, 'I
can't help it! She *makes* me say nasty things!'

FudgeMa sighs and stands. 'Kippers – ooo, SweetiePops?'

'What's that –? Oh, kippers! No, no, I'm too busy to eat, FudgeMa! I've got to keep my eye on the Makeover Queen of Vinegar Street! Watching! Watching! Watching!'

She's opening the curtains!

What? Oh, look! Where are my binoculars?

Behind the SpaceSpider.

Many thanks.

— **21** —

'Mandy Nylon has a glass of liquidized prunes for breakfast, Auntie Bruiser. Ugh! Give me kippers any day. And that was nearly an hour ago. And they're still sitting at the table. Mandy Nylon seems to be doing all the talking – Wait! I think she's – oh, where's the focus on these binoculars? – Yes! She's touching Mr Harmony's hand! Stroking it almost. What do you make of that?'

'Saddle sores 'n' spur blisters, DeputyPops, I don't make anything of it. Now why don't you stop all this darned foolishness. Your FudgeMa told me you haven't eaten a darned kipper all day –'

'Wait! Something's happening, Auntie Bruiser! Mandy Nylon's going upstairs – she's taking a glass of something up there! Must be more liquidized prunes. What's going on?'

'She must still be hungry, Deputy –'

'Oh, look at the way she wriggles as she walks. If we stuck a pair of maracas to her backside she'd pass for a rattlesnake. What's Mr Harmony up to . . .? He's still in the kitchen! Washing up the breakfast things. And he's . . . oh, mercy me, can you hear that? Mr Harmony's humming! Just like that woman! Honestly, I'll be chewing my way across the ceiling by sunset if that carries on – Aha! She's in her bedroom now! Look! Putting on one of her look-at-my-curvy-body dresses. I've seen more cloth in a tea-cosy. Now she's coming downstairs . . . Getting some black bin bags from under the sink – oh, what *is* going on?'

'Just have some kippers, Deputy –'

'Stop talking about kippers, Auntie Bruiser! How can I think about food when –? Look! The front door's opening. Mandy Nylon and Mr Harmony are stepping into the garden and they're – Oh, no! No! I don't believe! Auntie Bruiser! They're picking the weeds.'

'I can see that, DeputyPops.'

'Oh, the beautiful weeds! No! No! They're shoving them into those bin bags! How can they? And now they're – Oh, no! No! They're picking up all the treasure too! All the things I make my Creations with! Listen to them! They're calling it rubbish! Oh, do something, Auntie Bruiser! Stop her! Please stop her!'

'Wobbling wagonwheels, DeputyPops, I can't do that!'

'Why not?'

'It's *her* house!'

'But it's part of Vinegar Street, Auntie Bruiser! And every house on Vinegar Street has rubble and weeds in the garden.'

'But if she wants to *tidy* it –'

'*Ruin* it, you mean!'

'Suffering cactus, I hardly think she'll ruin –'

'Don't you care, Auntie Bruiser? Don't you love Vinegar Street as much as I do?'

'Well, of course I do, Deputy –'

'Then stop this garden mutilation!'

'But . . . I can't –'

'After *all* the things I've done for you, Auntie Bruiser! Who thought of a funeral for Old Gal? Me! Why, I even had to write the tombstone because you can't string two words together –'

'DeputyPops!'

'All your brave words and muscles – they don't mean a

thing. It's just an act!'

'DeputyPops!'

'You're not a cowboy!'

'Oh, please, DeputyPops. Please stop –'

'Cowboys are brave! A cowboy would help to save the street. But what do you do? Make excuses! You're not my friend any more! Hear me?'

'Oh . . . oh, how can you . . .?'

'You're nothing but a coward!'

'Oh . . . oh, DeputyPops!'

And suddenly Auntie Bruiser is rushing out of the bedroom, tears streaming down her cheeks.

— 22 —

That was nasty.

She deserved it.

No, she didn't.

But she wouldn't help me.

Poor Auntie Bruiser.

Well . . . oh, don't make me feel bad.

You deserve to feel bad. Poor Auntie Bruiser.

Oh . . . please. I'm sorry –

Tell her. Not me.

'Auntie Bruiser!' Poppy calls after her. 'I'm sorry! Please, I didn't mean it. I don't know what got into me! Please! It's that woman! She's making me say terrible things – Oh, that's the front door slamming!'

Too late now.

What do you mean?

Take a look.

Mandy Nylon has seen her! She's going over to my Auntie Bruiser.

'Peek-a-boo, Miss Bruiser. What a beautiful morning it isss – Why, what'sss wrong, Miss Bruiser? I do believe you're crying.'

'Suffering cactus, it's nothing.'

'Nothing! But you're upssset! Oh, I can't *bear* to sssee you like thisss. I jussst can't. Why don't you come inssside and share your ssstory with me? Mr Harmony, carry on with the weedsss and rubble, will you? I've got to have a heart-to-heart talk-show – I mean, gosssip!'

She's holding Auntie Bruiser's hand!

She's taking Auntie Bruiser towards No. 7!

And –

They've gone inside! This can't be happening! Where's my binoculars?

By your elbow.

Many thanks! Oh – look! Auntie Bruiser is sitting at the kitchen table. Mandy Nylon is putting the kettle on – and she's nodding so understandingly. So sympathetically! And ... oh, look! Auntie Bruiser has stopped crying. Mandy Nylon is touching her hand. And ... oh, Auntie Bruiser is smiling back.

Mandy Nylon's her friend now.

It can't get any worse.

You ain't seen nothing yet.

— 23 —

'Bruiserducks helped clear the weeds, you say?'

'Helped with *everything*, Uncle Larry.'

'And enjoyed it?'

'Mercy me, yes! After she'd had that little talk – or "talk show" as Mandy Nylon called it – the two of them came out and . . . oh, that wriggling walk of Mandy Nylon's! Honestly! We should attach one of your cocktail shakers to her backside, Uncle Larry. You'd have fresh cocktails all day. And then . . . Well, look! I've kept a record of the day so far.

10.30 – Auntie Bruiser starts helping Mandy Nylon and Mr Harmony clear garden of weeds and treasure.

11.00 – Mandy Nylon makes everyone cup of tea.

11.15 – Clearing of garden continues.

1.00 – Mandy Nylon makes everyone lunch. Tuna salad sandwiches on brown bread, followed by an apple.

2.00 – Clearing of garden continues.

2.30 – Mr Harmony starts taking black
bin bags full of weeds and
treasure away in car.
3.55 – Garden completely cleared. All
bags removed.
4.00 – Mandy Nylon makes Mr Harmony
and Auntie Bruiser a pot of
tea (no cake or biscuits).
4.30 – Everyone gets in Mr Harmony's
car and drives off.

'And that,' says Poppy, pointing at the clock, 'was nearly an hour ago. Where could they have gone, Uncle Larry? Where? Where?'

'I'm afraid I haven't the foggiest, my dear Poppyducks. It amazes me that so much has gone on while I slept the day away.'

'Well, you can't afford to sleep days away now, Uncle Larry. None of us can. Not with Mandy Nylon around. We've got to be alert and –'

They're coming back!

Where?

Down the street! Where do you think? Look out of the window.

Oh . . . yes! There's the car. And – what's that on the roof?

Tins of paint.

For . . . for the house!

Bingo!

Oh no! No!

'See them getting out of the car, Uncle Larry! Look how Auntie Bruiser is talking to Mandy Nylon. Like they've been friends for ever. And you see what they're taking from the car? Or, rather, what Mr Harmony and Auntie Bruiser are taking while Mandy Nylon watches. Paint! Brushes! Turps! And there's a ladder! Mr Harmony's propping the ladder against the house! You know what this means, Uncle Larry? The outside of the house is about to be painted –'

'Oh, please, Poppyducks! Do keep your voice down just a tad. I've still got a frightfully pounding headache!'

'Then you knocked back too many cocktails last night.'

'It was only a few –'

'Few dozen, you mean.'

'Well, really, Poppyducks, if a gentleman's not allowed the occasional nightcap –'

'Oh, stop waffling, Uncle Larry! Do something useful for a change! Get down there and tell Mandy Nylon she can't paint her house.'

'But . . . I can't possibly do that, Poppyducks.'

'Why not?'

'It's *her* house.'

'But it's part of Vinegar Street, Uncle Larry! And every house on Vinegar Street has peeling paint and cracks.'

'But if she wants to spruce it up –'

'*Ruin* it, you mean.'

'I don't think she'll –'

'Don't you care, Uncle Larry? Don't you love Vinegar Street as much as I do?'

'Naturally, Poppyducks –'

'Then stop this paint outrage!'

'But . . . I can't –'

'After all the things I've done for you. Shaking your cocktails until my wrists ache –'

'Poppyducks!'

'All your airs and graces and so-called fine breeding – it's all an act. There's nothing fine breeding in your veins. Know why? There's too much alcohol!'

'Oh, please, Poppyducks. Stop, I pray –'

'You're too sozzled to see what's happening beneath your very nose – your very *red* nose! You're not my friend any more. A friend would help me.'

'Oh . . . oh, how can you?'

'You're nothing but a drunk!'

And, suddenly, Uncle Larry is rushing out of the bedroom, tears streaming down his cheeks.

— 25 —

I repeat: That was nasty.

He deserved it.

I repeat: No, he didn't.

You like making me feel bad, don't you?

You deserve to *feel* bad. Poor Uncle Larry.

Oh . . . please. I'm sorry.

Tell him. Not me.

'Uncle Larry,' calls Poppy. 'I'm sorry! Please! I didn't mean it. I don't know what got into me! Please! It's that woman! She's making me say terrible things – Oh, that's the front door slamming!'

Too late now.

What do you mean?

Take a look.

Mandy Nylon has seen him. She's going over to my Uncle Larry . . .

'Peek-a-boo, Uncle Larry. What a beautiful afternoon it is – Why, what'sss wrong, Uncle Larry? I do believe you're crying.'

'It's . . . nothing at all.'

'Nothing? But you're upssset. Why don't you come inssside and share your ssstory with me. Miss Bruiser and Mr Harmony, carry on unloading the paint, will you? I've got to have a heart to heart talk-show – I mean, gosssip – with Uncle Larry.'

No! No!

Yes! Yes!

She's taking him to No. 7. They're going inside! Oh, this can't be happening again!

It's happening again all right – Before you ask, the binoculars are in your lap!

Many thanks – Oh, focus! Look! There! Uncle Larry is sitting at the kitchen table. Mandy Nylon is putting the kettle on – and she's nodding so . . . so sympathetically. And . . . oh, look! Uncle Larry has stopped crying. Mandy Nylon is touching his hand. Stroking it. And . . . oh, Uncle Larry is smiling.

History repeating itself, I'd say.

Mandy Nylon and Uncle Larry are friends.

You know what I'm going to say, don't you?

I ain't seen nothing yet?
Ten out of ten.

— 26 —

'It's been the worst day of my life, FudgeMa! First I called
Auntie Bruiser a coward and she went over to Mandy
Nylon. Then I called Uncle Larry a drunk and he did the
same! And I didn't mean to upset them! Honest! It's just

that – oh, mercy me, it's like I'm going a little crazy. And, of course, I felt even crazier when Uncle Larry came out and started to help paint the house! Look, FudgeMa, here's my notebook . . .'

5.45 – Uncle Larry helps Auntie Bruiser and Mr Harmony paint outside of house. Mandy Nylon bosses everyone around.

7.00 – Front of house finished. Sides of house start to get lick of paint.

8.00 – Sides of house finished. Mandy Nylon cooks dinner: grilled breast of chicken with steamed vegetables, followed by a low-fat yoghurt and fruit.

8.30 – Back of house starts to get painted. Can't actually see from my window, of course. But I can hear Mandy Nylon bossing everyone about.

9.00 – Mr Harmony and Mandy drive off in car.

'And that,' says Poppy, pointing at the clock, 'was thirty minutes ago. Where could they have gone at this time of night? And listen! Can you hear Auntie Bruiser and Uncle Larry at the back of the house? Still painting away! Mercy me, it's almost dark! They'll need torches soon.'

'Something eat – ooo – SweetiePops?' FudgeMa indicates the plate of vindaloo she's put on Poppy's desk. 'Nothing you've touched all day.'

'But I'm too worried to eat, FudgeMa. Just look at

what's happening to the house opposite. Garden cleared.
Window frames and window sills gloss white. And all the
walls – what colour is that? Magnolia, I think. Mercy me!
There might be a million shades of blue, but there's only
one shade of magnolia and it's called "Ugh!" ' Poppy runs
her fingers through her hair and rubs her bloodshot eyes.
'A single day! That's all it took, FudgeMa! To change No. 7
from a glorious building into a doll's house.'

Look out of the window.

They're coming back?

Ten out of ten!

'Look, FudgeMa! They're here! And – oh, what's all that
on top of Mr Harmony's car? Piles and piles of the stuff.
Like . . . like tiny rolls of carpet. The car's parking. Can
you hear Mandy Nylon humming, FudgeMa? Oh, it sets
my teeth on edge . . . Wait! What's that on the back seat?'

'Don't know, SweetiePops.'

'Oh, FudgeMa! You *must* know! What is that stuff?'

'Honestly don't – ooo – know, SweetiePops.'

'Oh, you're useless sometimes, FudgeMa!'

'Ooo . . . sweetie –'

'Well, you are! Just one question I ask you! That's all!
And can you help? No! You just sit there twittering "ooo".'

'Ooo –'

'There you go again! Honestly, FudgeMa, you must
have shares in a company called "Ooo" –'

'Ooo –'

'Stop it, FudgeMa! You drive me crazy sometimes! Hear
me? If I hear one more "ooo" they'll be putting me in a
straitjacket –'

And, suddenly, FudgeMa is rushing out of the room,
weeping.

Go on! Say it!

What?

Nasty!

Well, it was.

Oh . . . yes, I know! Oh, what's happening to me? I've never been like this before. I can hear FudgeMa sobbing in her bedroom. It's all your fault!

Me!?

You should have told me what they're taking from the car. Why torment me like that? Oh, I've got to apologize to FudgeMa –

No time for that.

What d'you mean?

Uncle Larry and Auntie Bruiser have appeared from behind the house. Look!

But what about FudgeMa?

Look!

Oh . . . Yes! Yes, I see. They've finished painting the back by the looks of it. Quick! Where's my notebook –

9.45 – Back of house completed. Now everyone is unpacking the stuff from Mr Harmony's car. They're taking it into the garden –

'It's flowers!' cries Poppy out loud. 'And turf!'

The very same.

Of course! I should have guessed. Now the house is finished, Mandy Nylon wants a . . . a . . .

Mmm?

A pretty garden!

— 28 —

Midnight —

Poppy is so tired she can barely write.

She slumps at the desk, clutching her pen. Watching the house opposite from beneath heavy eyelids as –

'There!' cries Mandy Nylon, clapping her hands with joy. 'All finissshed! Oh, jussst look at the houssse, everyone! It'sss ssso pretty! Oh, I'm getting tearful jussst looking at it! Jussst look at those nice neat rows of geraniums and marigolds! Oh, I will cry. I will, I will.'

'Don't cry, Mrs Nylon!'

'You mustn't, DeputyMandy!'

'You should be happy, Mandyducks.'

'Oh, but I am happy, everyone! These are tears of joy. Joy at my houssse! Joy at my garden! And joy at having sssuch dear friends like you! You've all worked ssso hard for me! Oh, I'm getting emotional again – A group hug, everyone!'

Oh, perr-lease! thinks Poppy, cringing. This must be the most sickly sight Vinegar Street has ever witnessed. Look at them! All hugging and saying they love each other – Oh, I can't watch any more! It's disgusting!

You're jealous really.

How can you –?

Only joking!

Not funny.

THE TRANSFORMATION OF NO. 7 IS COMPLETE.

Mr Harmony gets in the car and drives off. 'Missing you already, Mrs Nylon!'

Auntie Bruiser goes to No. 6. 'Missing you already, DeputyMandy!'

Uncle Larry goes to No. 4. 'Missing you already, Mandyducks!'

Mandy Nylon goes to No. 7. 'Missing you already, everyone!'

Where're my binoculars? Ah! Here! Oh no! Mandy Nylon's pulling all the curtains. Can't see anything! Lights are being turned off. She's obviously –

00.10 – Mandy Nylon goes to bed.

Oh . . . why keep on watching her? I'm seeing as much as everyone else and . . . well, they're all friends with her now anyway! I haven't proved anything. What's the point of this notebook?

To discover her secret.

Her . . . secret?

That's right.

You mean ... there's something more? More than just ... changing the house and garden? That's the proof you were talking about? A secret!

Yes.

Why don't you just tell me, TingleVoice?

You have to discover it yourself. Keep watching.

But I *have* been watching. And I haven't seen a thing.

You have.

I ... have? What?

A clue.

A clue to the secret! Oh, what clue? Tell me!

. . .

Please, TingleVoice.

. . .

Why won't you tell me?

You have to work it out for yourself.

Later.

Can't sleep! Been tossing and turning! Still thinking about what clue I've seen. Oh, where are my notes?

Later.

I've read and read my notes. But I can't see a clue. She's changed her house. That's all ... Oh, but it's not ... There's something else here ... Something I'm missing ... Some *clue* ... What? What?

I need some music to calm me.

The accordion's on your bed.

Oh, getting sleepy now . . .
Eyes heavyyy . . .
Sleeeeppp . . .

— 29 —

What's happening . . .? I'm on the ceiling!

I'm floating above my bed and looking down at –

Me! Twisted amongst the sheets. Fast asleep. I look worse than I feared. Bags under my eyes. And my hair looks like I've dusted the room with it.

Oh, my stomach's fluttering. Only . . . I'm not even sure if I've got a stomach. I can see right through me.

It's like I'm a ghost.

What a strange feeling! Head spinning a little bit.

Calm down. Deep breaths.

Only . . . well, I'm not even sure if I'm even breathing.

So this is what they call an 'out of body' experience. My astral body. I've read about this in books. Nothing to be afraid of.

So . . . well . . . let's make the most of it, I guess.

Let's see if I can move . . .

Think about the window –

Ah! There! If I think about the window and hold my hands out towards it then . . . well, I move towards it.

Or, rather, float towards it.

Or fly!

Flying! I'm flying!

Careful does it! I'm wobbling around a bit. If there was a Driving Test in Astral Body Experiences, I'd still need a few more lessons . . .

There! That's steadier . . .

Oh, the night air is billowing through my nightdress. Ruffling my hair. It's like I'm being caressed by the night itself. And everything seems so vivid. The moonlight is as blue as writing ink. The weeds smell like some exotic garden. And the insects – oh, I can hear every single chirrup and drone. Every wing fluttering –

And above – oh, above!

Look at the stars! An eternity of glimmering. Light years of orbits and eclipses. I can feel the whole cosmos vibrate and revolve around me. I'm adrift between insects and super-novas –

'Help!'

'Wh . . . what's that?'

A voice I've never heard before. So gentle. So . . . yearning –

'Help!'

Where's it coming from? I glide up and down Vinegar Street! Where are you? Where are you? It's not coming from Auntie Bruiser's house. I can see her through the bedroom window! Flat out across the mattress. Her face splattered with paint. Earth in her fingernails.

'Help!'

Where? Not coming from Uncle Larry's. I can see him through the bedroom window too. Tucked up beneath a feather eiderdown. Mercy me! I can smell the cocktails on his breath from here –

'Help!'

Oh, where? Where? Well, it's not coming from my house. Look! There's FudgeMa! Her cheeks still damp with tears. How could I have called her useless?

'Help!'

Behind me!

From No. 7.

I'll float towards the house.

'Help!'

It's coming from the back of the house!

I'll float there and –

'Help!'

The top window!

Can't see inside! It's only open a few inches and the curtains are drawn! But – mercy me! – I'm an astral body. Surely I can go through a window?

Well, let's see! Deep breath and –

Vsssshhhhh!

What a strange feeling. Like going through a warm shower.

'Help!'

Much louder now. But it's so dark. Can't make anything out. Wait for my eyes to get used to it . . .

Ah! There! Can just see the outline of a . . . bed!

And there's a figure in the bed.

Under a sheet . . .

'Help me!'

The figure's moaning in its sleep.

Oh, it sounds so sad. So lonely.

Closer . . .

The sheet's covering most of the figure's face. I can just make out . . . its nose and eyes! Perhaps I can get the figure to move. I'm going to stroke its nose with my astral fingers . . .

Stroooke!

There! The figure's moving a little. Oh, it's turning. The sheet is slipping. And the eyes are . . .

Oh, mercy me, the eyes are opening –

— 30 —

BRRRIIINNNGGGGGG!!!

Poppy's eyes click open.

BRRRIIINNGG!!

Turns alarm off.

Silence . . .

The secret! That's it! Mandy is hiding something – no,

not something! Some*one*! So ... what was the clue I'd seen? Tinglevoice?

. . .

The glass she took upstairs?

. . .

It was for that hidden person! Of course! But who is it? Who's she hiding?

. . .

I've got to find out myself. Right?

Bingo!

Then I will. I will!

What are you doing?

Going over there. The sun's only just risen. I've got a while before Mandy wakes up.

Fifteen seconds later.

Gently does it! Don't make a noise closing the front door behind me. There! Oh, everything smells damp and new. One or two bats flying over head. Insects. But, apart from that, silence . . .

Eleven seconds later.

I'm in No. 7's garden now. Feels so strange to walk on grass. Like shagpile carpet. Not that I've ever walked on shagpile carpet – but I imagine it feels like this. Look! Rows of geraniums and marigolds. So boring compared with the wild and multi-coloured weeds. And as for the magnolia paint ... well, that gets more 'Ugh' the closer you get. Now, creep round the back of the house and –

There it is! The window.

What you going to do?

Well, I can't shout out – that might wake Mandy up. Any suggestions?

. . .

You're as helpful as a hole in a lifeboat.

Thirty-three seconds later.

If I throw this handful of earth at the window, that might attract the attention of whoever's in there.

Good thinking.

No thanks to you.

Throw!

The earth makes gentle rapping noises against the glass.

Nothing!

Hasn't worked.

I can see that. What now? Look! The ladder. Lying flat on the ground. Perhaps I could lift it up to the window and –

Good idea . . . but –

But what?

I don't like to tell you this.

What?

Wait for it! Three, two, one –

'La-de-dah!'

Oh, no! Mandy Nylon's awake. It must be seven o'clock! I've got to run! Can't let her catch me hurling rocks at her secret –

Wait!

What now?

Look!

Where?

Up at the window!

A hand!

Poking out from under the curtain.

It's holding something –

'La-de-dah!'

Mandy might catch me any second.

Got to run –

The hand's thrown what it was holding.

Where?

There! Beside you!
A piece of screwed-up paper!
'La-de-dah!'
Can't look at it here! Back to my room! Quick! Quick!

Twenty-seven seconds later.
I'm sitting on my bed.
That was close!
Now, let's look at this piece of paper . . .

I LIKE YOUR MUSIC

— **31** —

'Wake up, FudgeMa!'
'Wh . . . what? – ooo!'
'Greetings! And look – breakfast in bed! Kippers with lashings of butter and a big pot of tea. Sit up, FudgeMa, so I can put the tray on your lap. There! Oh, FudgeMa, I'm so sorry I uttered such nastiness yesterday. Let's forget all about it, shall we?'
'Course of.'
'Thank you, FudgeMa! Now, eat up before your kippers get cold. And, while you're munching, let me tell you

what's been going on this morning.' Poppy takes a deep breath and continues. 'At seven o'clock this morning, Mandy Nylon got up and started her relentless humming. After that, Mandy Nylon did her jogging – or, perhaps I should say tripping and stumbling over the rubble – and, at eight o'clock, Mr Harmony turned up and the two of them had breakfast. So far, like yesterday. But *then*' – Poppy clutches FudgeMa's arm – 'things took a slightly different turn. Because Mandy Nylon and Mr Harmony left No. 7 and went to . . . Can you guess, FudgeMa?'

'Oh . . . er . . . ooo –'

'To No. 6! Yes! To Auntie Bruiser's! And then Uncle Larry left No. 4 and went there too. Now, I ask you, when was the last time Uncle Larry was up this early? Not since mammoths washed their tusks in the canal, I shouldn't wonder. Anyway, can you guess why they'd all congregated there, FudgeMa?'

'I . . . er . . . ooo –'

'To clear the garden! Yes, FudgeMa! What happened to Mandy Nylon's house is now happening to Auntie Bruiser's house. Of course, Mandy Nylon mainly just stands there giving orders – How're the kippers?'

'I . . . er . . . ooo –'

'FudgeMa,' says Poppy in a low, serious voice, 'I need your help.'

'Wh . . . wha –?'

'I need to break into Mandy Nylon's house – Please don't choke on a kipper, FudgeMa. I've got a reason. A very good reason. And I will explain – but not yet, FudgeMa. First I need to make sure my suspicions are correct. Let's just say I need to get into the house not for *my* sake, but for somebody else's. Will you help me, FudgeMa? Please say you will. Please! Please!'

'I . . . er . . . ooo –'

'Thank you, FudgeMa! I knew you wouldn't let me

down. Listen carefully! Here is GusPa's alarm clock. Take hold of it! Good! Now, this is what I want you to do . . .'

— 32 —

I'm peeking out from behind my front door.

Look at Auntie Bruiser and Uncle Larry. Laughing and putting their arms round Mandy Nylon. And Mr Harmony. What a disgusting sight – Ah! They're going into Auntie Bruiser's house for their elevenses. Time to make a dash –

I'm crossing the street.

Glance behind –

There's FudgeMa! At my bedroom window, clutching the alarm clock as instructed.

I'm sneaking to the back of No. 7 now and –

There! The ladder!

Oh, it's heavier than I thought! But I've got to . . . get it . . . up there to that window . . .

Just another shove . . .

Done it!

You there, TingleVoice?

I'm always here.

You're being very quiet.

You seem to be doing perfectly well without me. You going up the ladder or what?

Climbing . . .

Climbing . . .

My heart's beating like a tambourine! Can hear the blood pulse in my ears! Who's in the room? Who?

Outside the window now.

I rap the glass gently.

'Greetings in there,' I whisper.

Nothing.

Rap, rap.

And then . . .

A hand!

Sticking out through the gap at the bottom. It's holding yet another piece of paper.

I take it.

The hand goes back inside.

Carefully, I open the paper . . .

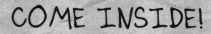

COME INSIDE!

— 33 —

I'm opening the window wider.

Curtains flap in my face.

Brush them aside.

Kick leg over.

Careful . . .

Other leg.

Flapping.

Brush –

In!

'Gr – greetings! I can't see you at the moment! My . . .
my eyes need to get used to the dark! I suppose there's a
reason you want it like this – Oh, I can hear you breathing.
You'd think I'd be scared, wouldn't you? But . . . well, I'm
not. Not a bit.'

Oh, what's this being put in my hand? Another piece of
paper. Hope I can see it . . . Let's see . . .

I'M ROCKY NYLON

Rocky Nyl– Oh! You mean –
Exactly!
It's her son!

— 34 —

'Rocky Nylon! Well . . . greetings once again, Rocky. I'm
Poppy Picklesticks from No. 1 Vinegar Street. A pleasure
to meet you. Even in this darkness. Mercy me, I'm a little
bit nervous, I don't mind admitting. After all, your mum is
bonkers – Well, what I mean is, I'm sure *you're* not
anything like your mum. Otherwise I'd *feel* it.'

Wouldn't I?

Perhaps.

Don't play games!

All right, all right ... He's nothing like his mum.

'Ah! My eyes are beginning to get used to it now. You're ... yes, you're sitting on the edge of the bed. And ... I'm not sure how old you are. Can't see your face. Oh, more paper ...'

I'M TWELVE YEARS AND ELEVEN MONTHS AND TWO DAYS.

'Precision! I'm like that too! Some people might think it's being a bit obsessive but, after all, there's a big difference between twelve years and one day and twelve years and three hundred and sixty-four days, so why simply say, "I'm twelve years old", unless, of course, it happens to be your birthday? Oh, I'm rambling now. I'm quite a chatterbox when I get going. Just tell me to shut up if I start to wear your eardrums out – Ah! More paper ...'

I LIKE THE WAY YOU TALK!

'Y – you do? Well . . . many thanks, Rocky. Oh, I can see
more now. You're wearing a . . . sky-blue tracksuit. And
you look like you've got a similar physique to mine. I tell
you, if I was a singer and stood behind a mike stand, you
wouldn't be able to see me! Ha! Ha! That was a joke,
Rocky. Oh, never mind. Ah! Can see more now. You're
tugging and pulling at your tracksuit. Are you nervous,

Rocky? Mercy me! You're trembling, Rocky! Oh . . . it's not me, is it? You're not nervous of . . . Rocky, if you want me to go I will! More paper . . .'

STAY!!

'Thank you, Rocky! I want to stay. Really I do – Ah! I can see your hair now. It's long, like mine and . . . oh, it's so blond. But the way you're sitting – with your head hanging down like that – it's covering your face! Oh, don't look away, Rocky! There's nothing to be shy of. Not with me. Won't you let me see your face, Rocky? Please! More paper . . .'

I LOOK RUBBISH.

'Mercy me! I'm sure that's not true! And . . . well, even if it were, what does it matter? You can have a nest of cockroaches up your nose and three green eyes for all I care. I just . . . I just want to see you, Rocky.'

Blond hair opens in front of his face like curtains –

'Mercy me!'

Those eyes – glistening like sapphires. The teeth – like pearls. His complexion – spun gold. Oh, my heart is pounding. I'm tingling all over. It's like an oven door's opened and stolen my breath. Can't speak. I just gaze into the fathomless blue of his eyes. His sad, sad eyes . . .

Say something.

I'm trying.

Try harder.

'Well . . . you're certainly not rubbish. In fact you're the most beaut–'

Get a grip, girl!

'– most pleasing to the eye, Rocky.'

I SAW YOU FLOATING IN MY ROOM LAST NIGHT

— 35 —

'You . . . you *saw* me!?'

A nod of the head.

'But . . . oh, Rocky, that was my out-of-body self. You know what that means? The astral me – I must have looked very strange! You must have been scared to death.'

A shake of the head.

'You weren't?'

Shake.

'Well, I'm sure you're just being polite, but many thanks anyway . . . Oh, you know what this means, Rocky? There must be some sort of connection between us. Yes! That's what was enticing me over here – Ouch! What's that I've just stumbled over? Looks like . . . why, they're dumb-bells. The sort bodybuilders use to build up their muscles.

Don't tell me you want muscles, Rocky?'

A vigorous shake.

'Then why . . .?'

MUM.

'Your *mum* wants you to have muscles? I've never heard anything so ridiculous in all my born days – Oh, look at you, Rocky! You're trembling with the need to tell me things. And, believe me, there's so many things I want to ask. I've got so many questions. Calm down, calm down. Don't overcook yourself, as FudgeMa would say.'

Rocky stops tugging at his clothes.

He's gazing at me.

What do I do now?

What do you want to do?

I want to . . . to . . .

Spit it out.

Sit . . . next to him.

Then ask.

Oh, I . . . I can't. What if he doesn't want me to?

Well, you won't find out unless you ask.

But . . . oh . . . I . . . I . . .

Take a deep breath and say it! I'll give you a countdown. Ready? Three, two, one —

'Can I sit on the bed, Rocky?'

A nod.

Easy, eh?

Oh . . . oh . . .

Go on!

— 94 —

'. . . Many thanks, Rocky. Now . . . Ah! There! I'm sitting! Now . . . why don't I ask you questions? And you can scribble or nod or shake your head. And that way you can begin to explain . . . things.' She looks round the gloomy room. 'I've never seen such a bare space. Just a bed, a wardrobe, a bedside cabinet. And the weights, of course. Very well – here goes!' A deep breath, then, 'Where's Mr Nylon, your dad?'

HE LEFT!

'How long ago?'

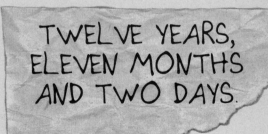

TWELVE YEARS, ELEVEN MONTHS AND TWO DAYS.

'So . . . he left when you were born?'

YES!

'Why, Rocky?'

'*Me.*'
'You! Why d'you say that?'
Rocky just stares.
'Well? Why –'
Scribble, scribble.

I DIDN'T SAY THAT!

'Nonsense! I distinctly heard you – Unless it was –'
No, not me.
Then who – Oh, wait! Don't say I –?
You did!
But I can't!
You can!
'Rocky!' gasps Poppy. 'I read your mind!'

— 36 —

Not sure how I feel about this. But . . . well, look at Rocky!
No doubting how he feels about it. He's grinning – oh,
those teeth! And looking at me with such excitement –
eyes so blue . . .

TRY IT AGAIN!

'You sure –?'

Big nod.

'Very well, Rocky. Let's do it! Now . . . Let's face each other a little more. That's right. Perfect. Now, let's begin with a simple thing. I'll ask you a question and you think of the answer. Understand?'

Nod.

'What's your favourite colour?'

Rocky frowns in concentration.

'nightstarmoonlightvelvetcloth I once had the cat I saw –'

'I got something but . . . oh, it was all jumbled. You've got to control your thoughts, Rocky. Understand?'

A serious nod.

'Try again.'

'I'd like a shirt like you're BLACK wearing that –'

'Wait! Black! Is that right?'

Big nod! Big smile! Big flash of eyes!

'All right, all right – stop bouncing up and down on the bed. You're making me quite seasick. But . . . oh, this is exciting. And black's my favourite colour too. Let's try again. And don't forget – control the thoughts! I'm still getting lots of other information too . . . What time of day do you prefer?'

'. . .'

'Think harder, Rocky.'

'Wheneveryone'sasleepNIGHT!'

'Night! And it's my favourite time too. Oh, Rocky!

You really are getting the hang of this now. And look at me – bouncing up and down like a lunatic too! Next question . . . What's your favourite month of the year?'

'*Kippers!*'

'Kippers! Mercy me! Is that after October or before?'

He's laughing.

I'm laughing too.

'Oh, Rocky! . . . Just imagine it! Having a birthday on the . . . twenty-fifth of Kippers! Ha-ha-ha!'

We're falling about on the bed now. Oh, my stomach hurts.

'*Kippers!*'

'Oh, stop it, Rocky! Stop it!'

BRRINNNNGGGG!

Suddenly, I jump to my feet, all laughter gone. 'That's my alarm clock! FudgeMa's been keeping watch. That's the signal your mum's on her way back –'

Click! Thump!

'La-de-dah!'

She's downstairs!

Rocky looks scared to death.

'Don't worry, Rocky! There's time to get down the ladder –'

I dash to the window.

'Farewell for now, Rocky!'

'*Fare – Quick!*'

And then –

'Oh, no! NO!'

'*What is it?*'

'It's the ladder, Rocky!' I gasp. 'It's gone!'

'*What we going to do? What? What? Wh–*'
   'Don't panic yet, Rocky!'
Footsteps on the stairs!
'Panic now, Rocky!'
Got to hide!
Look in wardrobe.
No! I'm too tall!
The bed!
Get to my knees.
Start scrambling under . . .
I whisper urgently, 'Get rid of the bits of paper! Quick!'
I'm scrambling, scrambling . . .
Rocky's rushing around picking up paper.
Footsteps!
Scrambling!
Picking!
   I'm almost under! It's a tight squeeze. Curl my legs up as far as possible. Hunch my shoulders! Ahhh – bedspring digging into my cheek!
   'Act natural!' I tell Rocky.
Rocky plonks himself on the bed.
Springs squish into my lips.
   I hear his nervous heartbeat reverberate through the metal –
   'Makeoversss!' Mandy Nylon's stilettoes click into the room. 'I jussst love them! Who needs a bottle of gin before breakfassst when a makeover can give you all the comfort

you require. Oh, I'm buzzing with it! Blood rushing! Oh, makeoversss! Nature'sss way of pleading, "Improve me!" ' Her stilettos come to a halt in front of Rocky. 'And then I have to come back here and sssee *you*!'

Rocky's trembling so much the bed's shaking.

'What a pathetic excussse for a ssson you are. Oh, don't look at me like that! Like sssome pathetic little animal! And ssstop that bottom lip quivering! You make me sssick! Sssick!'

I can't believe I'm hearing this. So this . . . this is the *real* Mandy Nylon. Poor Rocky!

'You're not the kind of ssson I wanted. I wanted a ssson with mussscles. Sssomeone who'd climb trees and play rough and come home with dirty fingernails and grazed knees. A bit of a bully with a wicked sssenssse of humour. A wild ssson. A thrilling ssson. Oh, that'sss the kind of ssson I dreamed of. That'sss the ssson your *dad* dreamed of. But when he looked into the cradle and sssaw you he cried, "What a thin, boring, feeble bag of bones." And he ran out of the hosssital never to be sssseen again. And I lossst the one man I'd ever loved. Because of you! Hear me? Because of you! You! You!'

— 38 —

Listen to her! I've never heard such craziness –

'And that'sss what it'sss been like ever sssince you were born. Every time I meet a man I like, he takesss one look at you and has a good vomit down the toilet. Then he walksss out crying, "What a feeble bag of bones" just like your dad did. No one can bear your rubbish looksss. And your rubbish voice! Well, it'sss going to ssstop. Hear me? It's going to ssstop!'

'*Shut up!*'

Oh, that's Rocky! Tell her, Rocky! Don't just *think* it! *Speak* it!

'Now here's another glasss of Macho Mussscle Build. Drink it all. Every lasst drop. And I hope you're doing your weight training. And don't forget to make your voice lesss crummy. Make it deeper. More like a proper ssson's.

After all, you don't want people to laugh at you, do you? – No! Don't ssspeak! I can't bear to hear you! And I'm going to cut your hair before you ssshow yourself in public. Look at it! You big girl's blousssse!'

'SHUT UP! SHUT UP!'

Tell her, Rocky! Don't think –

'I'm not having you ssscare away any more potential husssbandsss!' she shrieks, storming out of the room.

Slam!

And down the stairs and –

Slam!

– out of the house.

'I'm rubbish!'

— 39 —

'Don't think that!' I clamber out from under the bed. 'Your mum is the nastiest thing I've ever – Oh, Rocky! Don't cry. Please! I can't bear to see you curled up on the bed like that and –'

'I'm rubbish! Dad left because of me!'

'Oh, you don't really believe that, do you?' I rest my hand on the curve of his spine. Tiny bones tremble and click as sobs wrack his body. 'Your mum's lying. Men don't leave because of you. That's all gobbledegook. Even *I* can tell that.'

'Wh – what do you mean?'

'The men leave because of *her*.'

'But how can you know?'

'It's just so *obvious*, Rocky. Oh, the men might like her at first. All her brimming swirls and curls. But after a while . . . oh, she must drive them crazy. That's why they walk out. Nothing to do with you!'

'But people laugh at me –'

'No, Rocky! She's lying! I bet no one's ever laughed at you. And they certainly wouldn't here. Not on Vinegar Street. FudgeMa, Auntie Bruiser, Uncle Larry, they'd all think the same as me: that you're . . . you're beautiful, Rocky. There! I've said it! In fact, you're the most beautiful thing I've ever seen.'

'You . . . think so?'

I nod.

Slowly, Rocky sits up and, once again, his hair parts to reveal the treasures of his face.

'I like you just the way you are, Rocky. Don't change a thing. And as for muscles – well, honestly, who wants to walk around looking like a sock full of conkers?'

A giggle.

'Oh, I love the way you laugh – Why are you lifting that corner of carpet?'

'I want to show you something.'

'Floorboards?'

'No!' Another chuckle. 'These . . .'

'Mercy me! They're drawings! Fashion drawings! Oh, Rocky! Look at them! All these wonderful clothes you've been designing! Black dress with lace and sleeves like bat's wings. And this! Oh, look at this one! Black silk studded with stars and – oh, and this! A hat made to look like a nest with a raven on it! Oh, they're glorious! Is this what you want to do, Rocky? Design clothes?'

'Always.'

'And to think you have to hide these masterpieces. As if they're . . . something to be ashamed of. Oh, Rocky, don't you see your mum is wrong! Don't you see that?'

A slight nod.

'And deep down . . . you *know* she's lying about why all the men leave. Don't you, Rocky? Don't you?'

Another slight nod.

'Then say it, Rocky! I know you can talk if you want to. You mustn't be ashamed about your voice. Say, "My mum is wrong!" '

A pause.

'Please, Rocky.'

Then –

'My mum . . .'

'That's it, Rocky! Say it!'

'My mum is . . .'

'Oh, say it! Say it!

'My mum is wrong!'

'Louder!'

'MY MUM IS WRONG!'

'Louder! Louder!'

'MY MUM IS WRONG!'

And we start dancing round the room, laughing and chanting, 'My mum is wrong' over and over again.

Oh, Rocky's voice is so gentle and kind –

Danger!

Wh – what?

DANGER!

I stop dancing.

Mandy Nylon's listening!

But that's not possible. I heard her go –

You heard footsteps and the door slam.

'What's wrong, Poppy?'

'Oh, Rocky, I think your –'

'MUMMY'S HERE!!!' snarls Mandy, opening the bedroom door.

— 104 —

— 40 —

'Mum –!'

'Don't sssspeak! Your crummy voice makesss me cringe! And as for you –' Mandy glares at Poppy. 'Want to know how I knew you were in here? Your kipper and vindaloo ssstench. That'sss how! Now get out of my houssse and ssstop polluting my ssson with your disssgusssting ideasss –'

'Rocky's very talented!'

'Talented! Ha!' She picks up the drawings. 'They're the doodles of a big girl's blouse –'

'Don't rip them up!'

'I can rip what I like in my own houssse, little girl! Now you' – at Rocky – 'drink your Macho Mussscle Build and ssstart doing presss-upsss. And as for you' – at Poppy – 'out!'

'I'm not leaving Rocky!'

'OUT!'

'No!'

'OUT BEFORE I SSSTICK MY FINGERS UP YOUR NOSSSTRILS AND DRAG YOU OUT!'

'You . . . best go, Poppy.'

'UGH! THAT VOICE! SHUT UP! – AND YOU! LITTLE GIRL! OUT! OUT!'

'Don't worry, Rocky! I'll get help from Auntie Bruiser and Uncle Larry! Wait till they hear about this –'

'OOOUUUTTT!!!'

— 41 —

There they are! In the middle of the street. Wondering what all the shouting is about probably. Their faces and clothes even more splattered with paint. Leaves stuck in Uncle Larry's hair –

'She's a monster!' I pant, rushing up to them. 'A monster!'

'What ya darned talking about, DeputyPops?'

'Explain yourself, Poppyducks!'

'In there, Auntie Bruiser! The back room, Uncle Larry! Hidden away! Her poor son! His name's Rocky –'

'We know that!' says Mr Harmony, striding over. 'So you can stop all your sarcasm right now.'

'You . . . you *know*?'

'You bet your sweet patootie!'

'Sure do, DeputyPops.'

'Naturally, Poppyducks.'

Mandy has come out of the house now and is wagging her finger at Poppy. 'You sssilly little girl,' she says in her flossiest of candyfloss voices, 'I'm very angry with you.'

'What did she do, DeputyMandy?'

'Well, Misss Bruiser, if there was a jail in the ssstreet, our little Poppy would be in it! She – oh, I don't like to sssay it.'

'Say it, DeputyMandy.'

'Say it, Mandyducks.'

'Say it, Mrs Nylon.'

'Well,' sighs Mandy, running her hands over every curve in her wriggling body, 'I'm afraid she . . . broke into my houssse.'

'DeputyPops!'

'Poppyducks!'

'It's not true, Auntie Bruiser! It's not, Uncle Larry! Rocky asked me in.'

'Oh, really,' sighs Mandy. 'Sssuch lies from sssuch a cute little girl. My Rocky is far too shy to asssk anyone in. Haven't I shared that ssstory with all of you?'

'You have, DeputyMandy.'

'You have, Mandyducks.'

'You have, Mrs Nylon.'

'But he's *not* shy!' cries Poppy. 'Or, if he is, then she's *made* him that way. That poor boy's locked away in his room, ashamed of the way he looks. Ashamed of the way he sounds. And all because of her!' Pointing at Mandy Nylon. 'And she makes him drink Macho Muscle Build until he . . . conforms to *her* idea of a perfect son.'

'What imagination!' gasps Mandy. 'Miss Bruissser and Mr Larry told me you wrote ssstories but . . . oh, thisss one is jussst a little far-fetched, don't you think, little girl?'

'It's the truth!'

'I've already ssshared the ssstory of Rocky'sss – oh, how can I sssay – lack of confidence problem. The lasssst thing I want to do is pusssh him into the public gaze before he's ready –'

'LIAR!' yells Poppy.

Mandy's eyes brim with tears. 'Oh, why are you being ssso nasssty to me? Miss Bruissser, can you tell me? Mr Larry, can you? Mr Harmony, can you? Ah, Miss Fudge! There you are! Perhapsss you can explain! Why hasss your daughter taken an inssstant dissslike to me?'

'Because it saves time!' snaps Poppy.

FudgeMa puts her arms round Poppy.

'Oh, FudgeMa! Did you hear all this?'

'Yes, did I – ooo, yes.'

'And you believe me, don't you?'

'Always – ooo, yes!'

'And Auntie Bruiser? Uncle Larry? You've known me all my life! Have I ever lied? *Would* I lie? Never! And I'm telling you – this woman is destroying her son!'

'Ohhh!' cries Mandy, bursting into tears. 'A group hug? Please, everyone! I don't undersssstand – oh, oh, oh!'

Auntie Bruiser and Uncle Larry wrap their arms around Mandy and make gentle, comforting noises.

'You've gone too far this time, DeputyPops,' says

Auntie Bruiser, shooting a glance at Poppy. 'First you call me a coward and Uncle Larry here a darned drunk – and now this! Why, DeputyMandy is the most well-built and healthy-toothed filly I've ever seen this side of Texas. And for you to hurl such lies at her like this – Why, by scorpions and rattlesnakes, it's a darned shame!'

'Tell . . . tell her!' sobs Mandy, clutching on to Auntie Bruiser's arms. 'Tell her to ssstay away from my ssson.'

'DeputyPops! Stay away from Rocky Nylon. That's an order!'

— 42 —

Later, sitting on the sofa, Poppy hugs FudgeMa tighter than she's ever hugged her before.

'Oh, FudgeMa! What's happening to everyone?'

'Hush – ooo, SweetiePops.'

'Why are Auntie Bruiser and Uncle Larry acting like this? It's like Mandy Nylon has put them all under some kind of spell! And . . . oh, poor Rocky. He's up there! All alone with his torn drawings. And I want to comfort him. I want to help him. And . . . oh, FudgeMa, I miss him already! I miss him so much!'

PART FOUR

Sherbet Fever

It's been ten hours and fifty-nine minutes since I saw
Rocky.

That's six hundred and fifty-nine minutes.

Thirty-nine thousand, five hundred and forty seconds –

Correction: five hundred and forty-one seconds –

Two seconds!

Three seconds!

And each second feels like a minute. Each minute feels
like an hour. The hours days. And the days . . . oh, mercy
me, I can't even think of that. A whole day without Rocky.
It won't be possible. Without seeing him I'll . . . why, I'll
wither like an unwatered weed.

*You're sounding like something from a
soap opera.*

I know! Who would have thought it? Me!

*Didn't FudgeMa's vindaloo make you feel
any better?*

Couldn't eat a mouthful.

*Don't tell me! You just stared at the plate
and thought of Rocky.*

Precisely.

*The way he nervously tugged and pulled
at his tracksuit.*

Oh, don't torment me –

*Why don't you work on your SpaceSpider?
Look at it. On the desk in front of you –*

Oh, I couldn't! Nothing means anything without Rocky! What's the time?

One minute past midnight.

A new day!

That means – oh, I haven't seen Rocky since *yesterday*!

I keep thinking of that last look he gave me. So helpless. So lost.

I wish I could get a message to him somehow. Perhaps I'll just face the consequences and march across there and demand to–

Wait! What's this? A piece of paper in my dress pocket! Wonder what it –

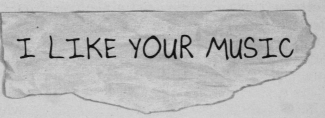

I LIKE YOUR MUSIC

Oh, it's Rocky's first message. More precious than the Dead Sea Scrolls –

Music! That's it! Rocky can hear my music! If I play . . . oh, it'll be my way of saying: I'm still here, Rocky! And I'm thinking of you! Oh, yes! Where's the accordion?

Hear it, Rocky! Hear –

'. . . *hear it, Poppy* . . .'

'It's Rocky! And . . . he's sending thought messages to me!'

— 44 —

'. . . *trying to make contact! All evening! Don't know if this has got through. Hoping your music will help* –'

It has, Rocky –

'*There's no way of knowing! You might be able to read my thoughts, but I can't read yours. Got an idea! Wow! Yes! Poppy, if you can hear me, play three notes!*'

Oh, you clever thing –

'*Wow! So fantastic! Oh, Poppy! I miss you! Do you miss me? Give one note for yes, two for no!*'

'*Wow! This is magic! I'm so sorry I didn't come out into the street when you were arguing. I was scared. Do you forgive me?*'

'Thank you, Poppy! I've been so upset ever since! Mum made me drink an extra glass of *Macho Muscle Build*. It was disgusting! I could smell vindaloo coming from your house. Smelt delicious. Wish I could have had that. Now, listen. I've got a bit of an idea. Want to hear it?'

♩

'You've got to go to sleep.'
Sleep! Oh, Rocky, what do you –?
'– then visit me as your astral body! Magic, eh? Don't forget, I saw your astral body the other night. Don't you think that's a magic idea?'

♩

'So . . . do it, Poppy! I can't wait to see you! Sleep! Sleep! Sleep!'

— 45 —

Impossible! I've been trying to sleep for one hour and fifteen minutes and . . . oh, I'm more awake than ever! I've tried everything: a big cup of cocoa, counted sheep (whoever thought of that one needs their brain tested) and I'm still restless enough to jog round the street. (Not that I would: I'm restless, not bonkers.)

Calm down! Relax! Unwind! Oh no! Now I'm reminded of Auntie Bruiser and Uncle Larry giving me an Emergency Headache Treatment! How could they side with Mandy against FudgeMa and me? What's got into them . . .?

I'm on the ceiling.
I'm asleep! It happened!
And look! There's me on the bed.
Mercy me! What a mess I look!
Quick! Let's get to Rocky!
Fly through the open window –
Oh, I've got so much more control than last night. I'd pass that Astral Body Experience Driving Test first go now –
There's Rocky's bedroom window.
It's open!
Float towards it . . .
And there's Rocky! He's sitting on the bed! Oh, the poor thing's been waiting all this time. My heart's beating so fast! How I want to see his face! How I want to hear his voice!
Through the window I go and –
'Greetings, Rocky!'
He doesn't move.
'Rocky! I'm here! Astral Poppy!'
Still nothing.
'Mercy me! Rocky! Rocky –'
He gets up and pokes his head out of the window, muttering, 'Hurry up! Please!'
'What do you mean, Rocky? I'm standing – or, I should say, hovering next to you! Oh, don't say you've lost the ability to see me! ROCKY! ROCKY! ROCK–'
He flinches!

Eyes dart around the room.
He heard something!
'ROCKY!'
'Poppy! Oh, wow! I . . . can hear you. But it's very faint!
Do it again! Louder! And stand in front of me! I'll
concentrate!'
'ROCKY!'
'Yyyy-esss! I saw something that time. Like a . . . fuzzy
TV picture!'
'ROCKY!'
'You're louder! Clearer!'
'ROCKY! ROCKY! ROCK–'

— 46 —

'Wow! Poppy! Wow! Wow!'

'You can see me?'

'Wow! Magic! Yes! I've been thinking of you all day.'

'And me you.'

'You have?'

'Yes, I couldn't eat –'

'Nor me! Or should I say finish my drink!'

'Bet your mum went bananas.'

'I don't care any more.'

'You don't?'

'No. All I care about is . . . well, you!'

'Oh, Rocky.'

'Oh, Pops – can I call you Pops?'

'I like it, Rocks – oh, can I call you Rocks?'

'I like it too – Oh, Pops! Look at us spinning round and round each other.'

'Best keep your voice down, Rocks! Don't want to wake your bonkers mum – oh, I've got so much to tell you, Rocks!'

'Me too, Pops.'

'I want to tell you all my favourite memories. And show you all my favourite things.'

'Me too, me too! – Look at this, Pops.'

'What, Rocks?'

'It's under the carpet – Here! Look!'

'A new drawing! How did you –'

'I've got some clean paper and pens hidden under the wardrobe.'

'Oh, it's truly glorious!'

'You think so?'

'A masterpiece!'

'Oh, Pops! No one's ever understood me like you.'

'And no one's ever understood me like you –'

Vsshhhhhh.

'Ooooo, Rocks!'

'Ooooo, Pops – what happened?'

'You walked right through me, silly!'

'Wow! What a magic feeling!'

'Do it again!'

'You sure?'

'Don't you want to?'

'Course I do –'

Vsshhhhhh.

'Oooo – best stop, Rocks! I'm getting quite giddy!'

'Me too. Nice though.'

'Oh, Rocks! I want to show you all my things too – Wait! How can I? My astral body's here but . . . oh, our real bodies are not supposed to meet . . .'

'There might be a way.'

'But, Rocks, your door's locked. There's no ladder –'

'I don't need the door or the ladder.'

'Then what –?'

'I'll use the window. Like you.'

'You mean –?'

'Exactly, Pops! Time for me to sleep and –'

'Astral travel!'

— 47 —

'Magic, eh?'
    'But . . . Rocky, do you think you can?'
    'Gotta try, Pops. OK – I'll lie on the bed! Get comfy!
Close my eyes . . .'
    'It's so difficult, Rocks –'
    'Never do it with you jibbering away, Pops.'
    'Sorry, Rocks.'
    Pause.
    'Asleep yet, Rocks?'
    'Don't think so.'
    'Tired?'
    'Not really.'
    'I told you it was difficult! It's like when someone says,
"Don't think of an elephant for the next sixty seconds!" All you
can think of are trunks and flapping ears! If someone says,
"Sleep!" then you're so busy thinking about –'
    'Zzzzz.'
    Mercy me! He's . . . he's done it! Oh, what a truly wonderful
thing! Look how calm and peaceful he looks. His hair is spread
across the pillow like a golden halo –
    Wait! This won't get him travelling! Got to encourage him!
Whisper in his ear –
    'It's Pops, Rocks. You're asleep. Now try to leave your body.
Think of . . . of a butterfly struggling out of its cocoon. That's it!
You're in a cocoon and you've got to get out to stretch your

wings. Out to where I am . . .'

'Zzzzz –'

'Try harder, Rocks! The astral world awaits. Get out of that cocoon. You can do it . . .'

Wait! Something's happening.

He's . . . blurring! Like the TV when it goes all double vision. Mercy me! There's two Rockys: one's asleep and the other . . . oh, the other is transparent. And glowing slightly –

'That's it, Rocky! You can do it!'

The astral Rocky is struggling away from the sleeping Rocky! It's floating up . . . up . . . up to the ceiling –

'Greetings, Astral Rocks!'

'Greetings, Astral Pops! – Wow! I did it!'

'Mercy me, yes! Come down here. Carefully though! You feel a bit wobbly at first!'

'Oh, Pops! You know what this means? We can go anywhere. No one can stop us, Pops!'

'No one can see us, Rocks – Oh, look! The sun's beginning to rise! This is our first dawn together, Rocks –'

BRRNNG –

'Oh, no! My alarm clock, Rocks! That means it'll –'

— 48 —

'– wake me up!'

BRRNNNGG –

Turn it off!

Silence.

Oh no! No! Just as our astral selves were making such plans. But . . . well, Rocky's still asleep. He can fly to me.

Rush to the window –

Oh, please think of it, Rocks. Come on! Float out of your window –

There! He's doing it!

Oh, look at him! Flicking hair from his eyes. Tugging at his tracksuit top. And his grin! So wide!

I wave.

He waves back and –

Wait! A noise –

'La-de-dah!'

Mandy's awake!

Mercy me, it's morning already.

Rocky shoots me an anxious look.

'Quick, Rocks!' I whisper. 'And – oh, be careful. Astral flying feels strange at first. There . . . oh, Rocks. You're a natural.'

Rocky hovers outside my window. *'Magic!'*

'But . . . oh, Rocks! Your mum'll wake you up any second –'

'No worries, Pops. We'll meet again. Tonight. You'll sleep. I'll sleep. And we'll have such magic. So enjoy being awake. Be happy, Pops. Because in dreams the street is –'

He disappears.

He's awake.

'– ours!' I finish for him. 'Oh, precisely, Rocks! In dreams the street is ours!'

— 49 —

I'm painting the SpaceSpider black.

Oh, how glorious it's looking . . . Yes! Yes! This is what it needed all along. So obvious. Why didn't I think of it before? Because there was no Rocky before. He's made my mind fizz and whizz like a firework! So many new ideas! Oh, Rocky –

'SweetiePops! Outside look! Houses damaged are mended being! Look! Come – ooo!'

'I'm too busy, FudgeMa.'

'There's workmen and – ooo – cement mixers –'

'Well, let the workmen and cement mixers get on with their jobs and let me get on with mine, FudgeMa.'

Wish FudgeMa would stop popping in and out of my room. It's so distracting when I'm trying to . . . Ah! Got it! I'll paint the red eyes on the dustbin lid –

'Oh, SweetiePops . . . outside is –'

'Stop overcooking, FudgeMa!'

Outside! Outside! Who cares?

All I care about is finishing the SpaceSpider by the time I go to –

– sleep!

Impossible.

It's twenty minutes past midnight. And am I tired? Not a bit. Despite a hot bath to relax me and three cups of cocoa –

'Greetings, Pops!'

'Rocks! You're here! The astral you! Oh, how can you get to sleep so easily?'

'Not sure really. Just close my eyes and – ping! Wow! Look at your room, Pops! All those books! Have you read them all?'

'Every one.'

'And your notebooks!'

'Full of stories, Rocks.'

'And all your Creations! Look at them! Wow! What's that on your desk?'

'It's called SpaceSpider.'

'It's magic! You're magic!'

'You're magic too, Rocks.'

'Really? No one's ever called me magic before – Wow! Is that your accordion?'

'Precisely, Rocks.'

'Wooowww!'

'It belonged to my GusPa.'

'Your dad?'

'Precisely.'

'Where is he now –? Oh, Pops, did he leave you like mine left me?'

'No, Rocks. GusPa died.'

'Oh . . . I'm sorry, Pops.'

'Many thanks, Rocks.'

'How long ago did . . . it happen?'

'Twelve years, nine months and twenty days ago.'

'Before you were born?'

'Three months before.'

'What did he look like?'

'He was tall and had large eyes – Look! This is his security pass from work. I keep it safe in this drawer. There's a photo of him.'

'Wow! He looks a bit like you, Pops.'

'That's what FudgeMa says too.'

'The same eyes . . . that magical look. It says Nuclear Power Plant across the top here. Is that where he worked?'

'Precisely, Rocks.'

'He wasn't a scientist, was he?'

'No, he was a security guard . . . He would sit in a little wooden cabin outside the main gates and . . . oh, I don't want to bore you with all this stuff.'

'Nothing about you is boring. I want to hear everything. Tell me – that's if you want to, Pops.'

'Oh, I want to, Rocks. I want to tell you every little thing about me. And this story . . . about my GusPa and how he met FudgeMa – it's the most glorious story I've ever heard.'

'Then tell me, Pops. Please. And don't miss anything out . . .'

— 51 —

'Well . . . oh, where to begin? I've got it! A taxi!'

'A taxi, Pops?'

'Precisely, Rocks. Because it was a taxi that brought FudgeMa here to Vinegar Street. She was the first person to move in. Oh, I can just imagine it. Seven brand new homes. All with "FOR SALE" signs outside. Except for No. 1, of course. Because that belonged to –'

'FudgeMa!'

'Her own house! Oh, how happy FudgeMa was that day. She told me that the whole street smelled so new. And it was so quiet. No neighbours then, you see. Just FudgeMa.'

'Bet she was lonely, Pops.'

'Not really, Rocks. You see, she was glad to get away from where she'd been living. People there took the mickey out of how she talked and what she wore – so, for the moment, being alone suited her just fine. Of course, she had a long trek to the city every time she needed some shopping. But FudgeMa didn't mind.'

'I suppose she had furniture delivered?'

'Well, she hardly carried it all on her back, Rocks – And then, late one night, FudgeMa hears some music.'

'Where's it coming from, Pops?'

'FudgeMa doesn't know. She goes into the garden. Oh, the music is so soft and gentle. It's the most beautiful sound she's ever heard. And it seems to be coming from –'

'*The Nuclear Power Plant!*'

'Precisely, Rocks. So FudgeMa starts walking across the wasteground. Even though she was only wearing her slippers and dressing gown.'

'*Hope it wasn't cold, Pops.*'

'It was a summer night, Rocks.'

'*Still could've been dangerous, Pops.*'

'She was very careful, Rocks. And I remember her telling me it was a full moon that night. And she could see her favourite star. The brightest star in the sky. Venus! Twinkling so bright. And then . . . oh, then, she sees –'

'*A wooden cabin, Pops?*'

'Precisely, Rocks.'

'*That's where the music is coming from, right?*'

'Precisely, Rocks! Because my GusPa's inside – although strictly speaking he's not my pa yet, you understand. And he's playing an accordion – that very accordion there! – and, as he plays . . . oh, FudgeMa tingles all over. She walks up to the cabin. GusPa is wearing a dark uniform. His eyes are large and dark. And he's, without doubt, the most beautiful thing FudgeMa has ever seen.

'GusPa asks, "Are you lost, madam?" '

'*And what does FudgeMa say, Pops!*'

'She can't speak, Rocks. She just swoons against the cabin window. Her breath mists the glass. GusPa rushes out and holds FudgeMa in his arms. GusPa is as tall and secure as a tree. Instinctively, FudgeMa reaches out and she touches his accordion. GusPa strokes FudgeMa's neck. She trembles like . . . something wounded. It was love at first sight, Rocks! Pure love!'

'*Wow! What happened next, Pops?*'

'FudgeMa and GusPa talked for hours and hours. All through the night, in fact. And – what's more – GusPa didn't have any trouble understanding FudgeMa at all. In the morning, GusPa went back with FudgeMa to No. 1 Vinegar Street and she cooked his favourite breakfast. Can you guess what it was, Rocks?'

'Kippers!'

'With lashings of butter. And that night she cooked his favourite dinner –'

'*Vindaloo!*'

'With garlic bread. And whenever GusPa asked FudgeMa what he could do for her, she told him, "Just your music play." And so he played. And, as he played ... well, time passed. Families moved in and out of Vinegar Street. And then, one day, FudgeMa said to GusPa, "Baby on way is – ooo!" '

'*You, Pops!*'

'Me, Rocks! FudgeMa and GusPa were so happy. To celebrate, FudgeMa cooked the biggest vindaloo ever. And GusPa played his accordion until his fingertips blistered. And later, they ... held each other, tingling with spices and tunefulness ...'

'*Why ... why're you looking so sad, Pops?*'

'Because the magic tingling didn't last long, Rocks. A few months later – oh, GusPa's death is so sad, Rocks.'

'*Don't tell me if you –*'

'No, Rocks! I want to tell you everything. If you want to know, that is?'

'*Of course I do, Pops. Tell me. How did ... your GusPa die?*'

— 52 —

'One afternoon ... FudgeMa is in the kitchen, chopping some onion for the vindaloo, when she hears a noise she's never heard before. It's like an electric scream! "WEEEE-AAAARR-WEEEE-AAARR!!!" it goes.'

'It's an alarm, Pops.'

'Precisely, Rocks.'

'From the Nuclear Power Plant?'

'Right again. FudgeMa rushes across the wasteground. She's still holding an onion in one hand and a chopping knife in the other. The alarm gets louder and louder. *"WEEE-AAARR!!"* And when she gets to the Nuclear Power Plant she sees . . .'

'What, Pops? What?'

'GusPa's cabin is empty.'

'Where's he gone?'

'She doesn't know.'

'Didn't she ask?'

'There was no one to ask, Rocks. The Nuclear Power Plant was deserted. On the big, iron gates was written, "CLOSED! KEEP AWAY! EXTREMELY DANGEROUS!" FudgeMa called out, "My Gus where is –? Ooo!" And she continued calling until the sun set. "MY GUS WHERE IS? MY GUS WHERE IS?" '

'Oh, Pops . . .'

'Day after day, FudgeMa sat in No. 1 Vinegar Street, crying. All she had left was GusPa's alarm clock and his accordion. He hadn't taken it in that day, you see. FudgeMa tried to play it. But in her hands the thing just wheezed and moaned like a dying animal.'

'What a sad story, Pops –'

'It's not quite over yet, Rocks . . . One day FudgeMa opened the front door and there was a plastic bag on the doorstep.'

'A shopping bag?'

'No, much smaller. Like a . . . like a packet of cup-a-soup. And attached to it was a letter.'

'What did the letter say, Pops?'

'It said – well, here! I keep it safe in this drawer too. Read it for yourself, Rocks . . .'

Dear Occupant of No. 1, Vinegar Street,
   I understand you were quite close
to Security Guard No. 2211121141115.
As there are no known relatives, we
thought you might like to dispose of
his remains. They are in the bag
provided.
   May I take this opportunity to
offer my sincere condolences for your
loss. But, unfortunately, accidents
like this can happen in any business.
   The Nuclear Power Plant is now
abandoned and will soon be encased in
a thick layer of concrete.
   It's advisable not to crack this
concrete for another ten thousand
years or so. Otherwise you'll cause a
chain reaction that will result in
the end of the world.

Yours sincerely

Mr N P Plant

MR NUCLEAR POWER PLANT

P.S. I also enclose his Security Pass
as a memento.

— 53 —

'Oh, Pops . . . that's terrible.'

'It is, Rocks.'

'What did FudgeMa do?'

'What could she do, Rocks? Except live alone and weep. Days turned to weeks. Weeks became months. And then . . . well, Auntie Bruiser moved into the street. Although, of course, she wasn't my Auntie Bruiser then.'

'So, FudgeMa had a friend, Pops.'

'She did, Rocks. And, one day, FudgeMa decided to have a funeral for GusPa. So she hopped on Auntie Bruiser's motorbike – or Old Gal, as it was known – and they drove across the wasteground to the Nuclear Power Plant.

' "This is where I first my SweetieGus met – ooo, SweetieBruiser," ' FudgeMa told Auntie Bruiser.

' "Be brave, DeputyFudge," said Auntie Bruiser.

'And FudgeMa climbed up a metal staircase to the top of the concrete-covered building.

' "Goodbye – ooo – SweetieGus!" she cried.

'And she cast his ashes to the wind. And the wind picked them up and scattered them all over the wasteground and . . . oh, all over the street.'

'Don't get upset, Pops.'

'I'm all right, Rocks. Really. It's just that . . . well, I've thought these things so much. And I've even written it down – I'm sure it'll make a glorious novel one day – but

I've never . . . well, I've never actually *told* it to anyone before.'

'*Wow! I'm honoured, Pops.*'

'Anything for you, Rocks.'

'*Then . . . well, will you play the accordion for me? I just love it. Please!*'

'Of course, Rocks. But . . . well, not here. Might wake FudgeMa. Might even wake *you* up –'

'*Then where, Pops?*'

'Follow me! We'll sneak out the back of the house. And go down to the –'

— **54** —

'The canal! Don't you think it's beautiful, Rocks? Look at the way the moonlight glimmers on the green slime and rats swim round rusty supermarket trolleys! And there! Frogs! Oh, you can keep the Tropical Rain Forest – give me the canal any time! Now, I'll just sit among these glorious weeds and . . .'

'*Wow! Magic, Pops.*'

'Can . . . can I ask you something, Rocks?'

'*Anything, Pops.*'

'Has your mum always been . . . well, bonkers?'

'She's always been a bit bonkers, I guess. But . . . well, the bonkers level has been getting worse and worse.'

'Tell me about it, Rocks. Please. I want to know everything.'

'Wow! I've never really talked about this . . . Don't know where to begin, Pops.'

'Begin with your dad, Rocks.'

'What about him?'

'Well, what was he like?'

'Never seen him, Pops.'

'But your mum must have mentioned him.'

'Well, yes. She . . . she told me how they met.'

'Oh, tell me, Rocks.'

'Won't tell it as good as you, Pops. Not magic with words like you.'

'Of course you are, Rocks.'

'Well . . . they met in a pub. Mum was a barmaid. And Dad would come in for a pint of beer and a bag of pork scratchings. He'd wink at Mum and crack jokes. And Mum'd wink back and giggle. And . . . oh, I'm not very good at this?'

'You're doing gloriously, Rocks.'

'Wow! Thanks, Pops. Well . . . yes! That's it! One day, Dad said to Mum, "Wanna watch me play football this Sunday?" And she said, "Yes." Dad loved football. He played it over the park with his mates.'

'So your mum went to watch?'

'She did, Pops. And Dad scored seven goals. And every time he scored, Mum yelled, "Goal!" at the top of her voice. Afterwards . . . she gave him a big hug. He smelled of crushed grass and there were grazes on his knees. And as Mum hugged him, she fell in love.'

'That's glorious, Rocks.'

'Wow! Thanks, Pops – Oh, keep playing your music, Pops. It . . . it inspires me.'

— 55 —

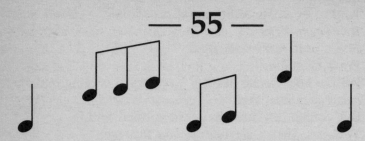

'*Mum loved Dad more than anything, I think. But . . . well, you know what happened next. When I was born, Dad left.*'

'Because of your mum, not you, Rocks.'

'*Oh . . . I've always known that, Pops . . . Deep down, Especially as . . . well, I've seen it in action.*'

'What do you mean, Rocks?'

'*With all the boyfriends Mum has had since. She meets someone – and he's always the same type . . . you know, with muscles and a loud mouth and a flash car –*'

'Who likes football!'

'*And beer and pork scratchings.*'

'And calls her "pretty" all the time.'

'*Exactly, Pops! Wow! How did you know?*'

'Not hard to guess, Rocks. Prettiness is your mum's nuclear weapon. All those curls and curves and skin-tight dresses. It can have an effect on people. Mercy me, look what she's done to Auntie Bruiser and Uncle Larry. Not to mention Mr Harmony. They're all . . . well, hypnotized by her.'

'*The hypnosis doesn't last long, Pops. Once they get bored with the prettiness . . . well, they leave.*'

'And that's what happened with all her boyfriends.'

'*Every one! Sometimes it'd last a week. Sometimes a month*' or two. They'd go out dancing every night. He'd buy her flowers and chocolates. And then – Bahm! She's dumped.'

'And your mum would blame you!'

'Every time.'

'And she gets more bonkers.'

'Right again! Every time a bloke clears off, she tries to make herself . . . well, more perfect.'

'Perfect? According to who?'

'All the telly chat shows she watches. You know the ones! How to give yourself a perfect figure. A perfect hairstyle. Perfect house –'

'The Makeover Queen!'

'That's my mum!'

'Oh, I knew there was something . . . something worrying about your mum. Even before I'd seen her. Before she moved in. From the moment Mr Harmony wrote "SOLD" on the "FOR SALE" sign.'

'But how, Pops? You know so much. You even knew Mum was hiding me in my bedroom. How?'

'Well, it's partly common sense, Rocks. But mainly, it's because of . . .'

'What, Pops?'

'. . . TingleVoice.'

— 56 —

'TingleVoice? What's that?'

'It's inside me. It's . . . oh, I don't know how to describe it, Rocks. I've never talked about it before. Not to Auntie

Bruiser or Uncle Larry. Not even to FudgeMa.'

'*Oh, try, Pops. Please.*'

'Well ... I've always had this feeling inside me. A tingling feeling. And sometimes ... well, it tells me things.'

'*What sort of things, Pops?*'

'Well, like a few months ago. FudgeMa couldn't find her fan anywhere. And it's a glorious thing. A present from Uncle Larry. FudgeMa searched all over the place. She was so upset thinking she'd lost it. And then – out of the blue – the tingling feeling inside me made me blurt out, "Freezer!" And when we looked – well, there it was. Tucked between some frozen kippers and a bag of vindaloo.'

'*Wow! Magic, Pops.*'

'And there's lots of other examples. Like when we were all having a picnic in the wilderness – oh, you'd love it out there, Rocks! You can feed the bats.'

'*Bats!*'

'Yes! They nest in the Nuclear Power Plant. There's hundreds of them. Thousands. Anyway, we were having a picnic and suddenly the tingle told me, "Rain". So I told everyone to pack up and, believe me, we got home just in time.'

'*It rained, Pops?*'

'Enough to warrant Ark building, Rocks.'

'*Wow! So this ... TingleVoice told you about me?*'

'Well, it told me something was wrong. That your bonkers mum had a secret. And it's been telling me more and more lately. In fact, I've only just started calling it TingleVoice. And asking it questions.'

'*Asking it questions, Pops?*'

'Well ... yes. You see, up until recently I had no control over it. I never knew when it was going to tingle me anything. And sometimes it would tingle me things I *didn't* want to know and tingle me nothing about things I *did* want to know. But lately . . .'

'*You've been controlling it more?*'

'I think so, Rocks.'

'*Wow! Magic! – And look, Pops! Oh, look! The frogs!*'

'Mercy me! They're jumping out of the canal.'

'*Jumping closer, Pops.*'

'And croaking louder, Rocks.'

'*And look! There! Rats!*'

'Crawling closer, Rocks.'

'*Squeaking louder, Pops.*'

'Look at their long, pink tails, glistening!'

'*And there! Look, Pops.*'

'Spiders, Rocks.'

'*They're all gathering round us, Pops.*'

'Mercy me! You know what they're doing, don't you, Rocks.'

'*What, Pops?*'

'They're listening to the music!'

'*Magic, Pops!*'

'Magic, Rocks!'

'*Keep playing, Pops!*'

'Oh, Rocks! How glorious this is! You hovering near by. A gentle breeze . . . Moonlight . . . Starlight . . . And all my favourite animals nearby . . . I had a pet spider once . . . When it died I buried it . . . in a . . . a . . . match . . . boooxxx . . .'

— 57 —

I'm floating!

'Greetings, Astral Pops!'

'Greetings, Astral Rocks! And . . . oh, look at the sleeping me. Surrounded by animals. There's even a frog on my accordion.'

'Does that bother you, Pops?'

'Not at all, Rocks!'

'Let's fly, Pops!'

'Fly, Rocks! – Oh, look at us! Zooming across the surface of the canal! So fast! Now up –'

'Up!'

'Oh, amazing!'

'Amazing!'

'Higher, Rocks!'

'How high, Pops?'

'Mercy me . . . I don't know! Just keep going! Up and up!'

'Up! Up! Look, Pops! The brightest star! Is that –?'

'Yes, Rocks! It's Venus.'

'Your FudgeMa's favourite.'

'Mine too, Rocks!'

'Mine too, Pops!'

'Look, Rocks! Out there! The Nuclear Power Plant! How truly majestic it looks! Like an ancient temple –'

Vsssssshh!

'Rocks! You surprised me! And . . . mercy me, when an astral body flies through another astral body, the sensation is twice as

strong! Try it again!'

VSSSSSHHHH!!

'Mercy me!'

'Wow!'

*'And look, Rocks! Far below us! Vinegar Street! So small!
Like toy houses! And . . . Oh, mercy me! Wait! Look! The street
looks . . . totally different! Quick, Rocks! Back down! Faster . . .
Faster . . . Oh, look! What's happened to Vinegar Street? I knew
that Auntie Bruiser and Uncle Larry were having their houses
done like your mum's. But – the other three! The ruined houses!
Nos. 2, 3 and 5! Look! They've been . . . rebuilt.'*

'Didn't you know, Pops?'

*'No! I was so busy finishing the SpaceSpider and thinking
about – Oh, FudgeMa! This is what she was trying to tell me!*

about – Oh, FudgeMa! This is what she was trying to tell me! The workmen! The cement mixers! Mercy me, every house is neat. And painted magnolia. With neat lawns. Neat rows of geraniums. Marigolds. And – the street too! No weeds! No . . . no nothing! Everything is so tidy and antiseptic! Oh, Rocky! Rocky! Everything's changed!'

'Except your house, of course.'

'My house! The only one as it used to be! Poor FudgeMa! No wonder she was so upset! Looking out of the window and seeing this . . . this nightmare unfold!'

'That's not all, Pops! Do you know who's living in No. 2?'

Ping!

He's disappeared!

Look – the sun's risen! His mum must have woken him up –

— 58 —

What woke me?

Oh, a frog on my face!

Brush it off.

And quick – to the street! What did Rocky mean? Who's living at No. 2? Next door to me?

Wait!

I couldn't see it from above but – there!

Parked outside No. 2.

That looks like Mr Harmony's car. What's that doing there?

Can't you guess?

Oh, there you are, TingleVoice. Thought you'd gone on

holiday. Well, make yourself useful now you're back. Tell me why Mr Harmony's car is –?

He's your new neighbour.

He's my . . . oh, no! It can't be! You sure?

Sure.

Mr Harmony living at No. 2 –

No time to brood. Things are about to happen. You ready? Three, two, one –

Lights go on in No. 7.

Lights go on in No. 6.

Lights go on in No. 4.

Lights go on in No. 2.

Wh . . . what's going on? Everyone's getting up at the same time. And –

'La-de-dah . . .' goes Mandy Nylon.

'La-de-dah . . .' goes Auntie Bruiser.

'La-de-dah . . .' goes Uncle Larry.

'La-de-dah . . .' goes Mr Harmony.

No! They're all humming! I can see them in their kitchens! They're all wearing tracksuits! Don't tell me they're going to –

You got it!

Oh no!

Mandy Nylon comes out and jogs to No. 6.

Auntie Bruiser comes out of No. 6 and jogs with Mandy Nylon to No. 4.

Uncle Larry comes out of No. 4 and jogs with Mandy Nylon and Auntie Bruiser to No. 2.

Mr Harmony comes out of No. 2 and jogs with Mandy Nylon, Auntie Bruiser and Uncle Larry around the street.

'Stop it!' cries Poppy. 'Wh– what are you doing?'

'Ignore her, people!' instructs Mandy. 'If she can't be one of usss then she'sss not worth talking to.'

'Auntie Bruiser? Uncle Larry? Don't listen to her!'

'Sorry, DeputyPops –'

'Sorry, Poppyducks –'

'You heard Mrs Nylon, everyone,' says Mr Harmony. 'No talking to the weirdo.' Then he points at Poppy. 'You've only got yourself to blame! You and your weirdo mother! Conform or –'

'Or what, baldy?' snaps Poppy.

'Oh, the offensssivenesss of her,' sighs Mandy Nylon. 'Don't wassste your breath arguing, Mr Harmony. Come on, people! Three more lapsss!'

Jog, jog, jog.

'Conform or what?' Poppy yells after them. 'Conform or –'

Today's the day!

Wh– what day?

It will happen!

What will?

Everything!

— 59 —

'Oh, forgive me, FudgeMa! I should have listened to you. You tried to warn me. But what did I do? Ignore you! I was too wrapped up in my own little world! And now look at us! Peering through the living room curtains at – at what, FudgeMa? It doesn't look like Vinegar Street any more.'

'Oh, know I – ooo, SweetiePops.'

'What's the time – oh, it's four minutes past eleven! I bet they're all doing housework! Yes! I can hear vacuum cleaners and washing machines! Mercy me! This is what it's going to be like from now on, FudgeMa! They're all going to copy Mandy Nylon! Up at seven! Jogging! Liquidized prunes for breakfast! Housework! – And look! Look! It's her, FudgeMa! Leaving No. 7. Still wearing another one of her stitch-and-a-wish dresses. More make-up than a truck-load of clowns. Hair full of waves and curls – oh, look at the wiggly, silly walk! The more I see her, the more I want to throw up . . . She's going to Auntie Bruiser's. She's knocking. Door's opening. And – oh, look, FudgeMa! It can't be! Look! Look!'

'I believe it don't, SweetiePops!'

'Nor do I, FudgeMa! But it's true! Auntie Bruiser is wearing a dress! Just like Mandy's! And stilettos! Just like Mandy's! And a wig! Just like Mandy's! And – oh, look – AUNTIE BRUISER IS A MANDY CLONE!!'

— 60 —

'Now they're going to Uncle Larry's, FudgeMa! Auntie Bruiser's walking like Mandy too. I can hear them "la-de-dahing" from here! Mandy's knocking. Uncle Larry's opening the door. And – oh, look! The nightmare's increasing! Uncle Larry is a Mr Harmony clone. Suit! Wig! She's turning everyone into her idea of perfect people! Oh, FudgeMa! It's the most horrific thing I've ever seen – They're coming this way! Don't hide, FudgeMa! This is our house. We're not doing anything wrong! FudgeMa!

Fudge–'

Knock-knock!

'Help – ooo – SweetiePops.'

'Mercy me, FudgeMa! I refuse to be scared by a bunch of wig-wearing, air-headed, la-de-dahing, prune-eating joggers!'

Knock –

'I'M COMING! – Wait here, Fudge-Ma! I'll deal with them . . . Now, what do you lot want?'

— **61** —

'What rudeness from sssuch a potentially cute –'

'Cut the waffle, peroxide bonce!'

'Stop that sarcasm right now –'

'It wasn't sarcasm! It was an insult. Get your facts right, baldy!'

'DeputyPops!'

'Poppyducks!'

'And as for you two – Look at you! My own Auntie Bruiser and Uncle Larry – clones!'

'Shut it!' Mandy suddenly steps forward and glares up at Poppy. 'Now lisssten carefully, little girl. We are here as the V.S.S.F. That ssstands for the Vinegar Ssstreet Sssuitability Force. Our aim is to make sure everyone lucky enough to live in Vinegar Ssstreet complies with what the majority consssider to be sssuitable. And we – that'sss me, Miss Bruissser, Mr Larry and Mr Harmony – are the majority. And you' – jabbing a finger at Poppy –

'are the minority. With me ssso far?'

'. . . Mmm,' replies Poppy.

'As the President of the V.S.S.F., it'sss my duty to inform you that No. 1 Vinegar Ssstreet isss, at the moment, unsssuitable in many waysss. If these offencesss –'

'Offences!'

'– continue, they will be dealt with in the mossst

sssevere way. We have prepared a lissst of the offencesss and how you can correct yourssselves.'

'Correct ourselves! Mercy me! I've heard about enough of this. It's *you* who are offensive. Now leave us alone! And you can shove your list up your suitabilities!'

Poppy slams the door.

Gasps of outrage from outside!

Then –

The list is put through the letterbox.

'You have sssix hours to ceassse your offencesss,' Mandy snarls through the letterbox. 'Think about it, little girl!'

— 62 —

THE VINEGAR STREET SUITABILITY FORCE
OFFICIAL WARNING TO NO. 1 VINEGAR STREET

OCCUPANTS: Fudge Picklesticks
           Poppy Picklesticks

You have been found guilty of the following offences:
1) Not having a magnolia house.
2) Not having geraniums and marigolds in the garden.

3) Not waking at 7.00.
4) Not eating liquidized prunes for breakfast.
5) Not jogging.
6) Not doing housework.
7) Not eating tuna sandwiches and yoghurt for lunch.
8) Not going 'la-de-dah'.
9) Not wearing suitable clothes.
10) Not having suitable hairstyles.
11) Cooking pongy food.
12) Playing music at night.
13) Breaking into No. 7.
14) Talking to Rocky Nylon.
15) Telling lies about Rocky Nylon.

'This is too much, FudgeMa! I'm so annoyed! Look at me! Trembling! That woman! You know what this means? Can't eat kippers or vindaloo! Can't wear these clothes! Can't play GusPa's accordion! Can't ever meet Rocky – Oh, it's an outrage! Really it is! FudgeMa – stop hiding under the table.'

'Oh . . . could how SweetieBruiser and SweetieLarry?'

'Please don't cry, FudgeMa!'

'My dear friends . . . so happy was I once . . . Happy so!'

'That's it! I've had enough! I'm going to tell Mandy Nylon exactly what she can do with her "Official Warning"! I'm not having us hiding like hunted animals –'

Careful!

I don't care!

But –

No, TingleVoice. This has gone too far. And it's going to stop.

— 63 —

'Open up! No. 7 Vinegar Street! You hear me in there? Open this door! Oh, I can hear you. All in there, are you? Having a big group hug? Chattering away and going, "La-de-dah". Talking about me and FudgeMa, eh? How you've won? How you think we're going to start planting geraniums and eating prunes? Well, you're wrong! Hear that? W-R-O-N-G! FudgeMa was the first person on this street! No one's going to tell her – or me – how we should live! So – here! I'm tearing your precious "Official Warning" into pieces and I'm shoving it through your letterbox. Oh, another thing! *Nothing* will *ever* stop me meeting Rocky! We have ways of communicating you can't even dream of! So "la-de-dah" to the lot of you! I'm going home now! And if any of you so much as touch a weed in my garden, I won't be responsible for my actions! Farewell! ... FUDGEMA! START COOKING THAT VINDALOO! AND MAKE IT EXTRA PONGY!'

'More garlic bread – ooo – SweetiePops?'

'Many thanks, FudgeMa.'

'Vindaloo – ooo –?'

'Many thanks – oh, what's that? A letter, I think – Yes! Don't bother yourself, FudgeMa. I'll get it.'

'Ooo, SweetiePops! Worried I am still.'

'This is *our* house! *Our* lives! There's nothing the so-called Vinegar Street Suitability Force can do to change us. Now, let's see what this newsletter's about. Wouldn't surprise me if it's an apology, FudgeMa.'

Here it is! It's addressed to 'The Occupants of No. 1'. Open it –

NOTICE OF EVICTION

Wh– What? Eviction! What are they talking about?

```
Dear No. 1,
   As you know, the house in which you
are living is Leasehold not Freehold.
This means you only have it for a
certain number of years. Your lease
was for 10 years. This expired some
time ago.
   The decision whether or not to
extend your lease is taken by the
```

Vinegar Street Suitability Force. At a
recent meeting, it was unanimously
decided, by all members of the
Suitability Force, that you are no
longer suitable.

   You have until tomorrow morning to
get out and never show your faces in
Vinegar Street again.

Signed

Mr Harmony

Mr Harmony
Landlord of the Community of Harmony

But they can't!
Can't
They won't!
Will!

.

— 65 —

Evicted! Me and FudgeMa? Out on the streets! Banished!
Away from the street! The house where I was born! The
canal! The wasteground! The bats! Rocky! Oh, Rocky! –
No! I won't let it happen –
   'What's say the letter – ooo, SweetiePops?'

'Oh – nothing, FudgeMa! Don't worry.'

Won't tell FudgeMa! I'll deal with this myself!

Rip!

You're tearing the letter into pieces!

Rip! Rip! Rip!

What are you going to do now?

I'm going to teach them a lesson, TingleVoice! You hear me?

Loud and clear.

A lesson they'll never forget.

When?

TONIGHT!

— PART FIVE —

Space Spider

— 66 —

Moonlight.
Starlight.
Insects.
Poppy sits cross-legged on her bed.
She gets the accordion strapped on.
In front of her is the SpaceSpider.
You ready?
I am.
Focus on the power inside you.
I know, I know.
*You always knew it was there, didn't you?
Your power — Ah! Feel that?*
Yes! Like an electric current inside me.
Focus!
I am!
Now play . . .

That's Pops! thinks Rocky, lying on his bed. Wow, I just love her music. Mustn't let it distract me though. Want to get to sleep early tonight. Can't wait to talk to Pops about

what's been going on today! Heard Pops shouting. So . . .
sleep! Oh, come on! Sleep . . . Sleep . . . Slee–

– eep!
Done it! Wow! Quicker than ever!
Now, out of the window! Fly round the house – oh, there's
Mum! In her room! Look at her! Grinning at her reflection!
Wonder what she's thinking. Who cares? Pops! Pops! Here I
come –

The SpaceSpider begins to tremble.
   Doll's arms round the edge, quivering as if alive.
   That's it!
Yes! Yes!
Keep playing!

Outside, the insects buzz louder.
Frogs croak louder.
Spiders crawl faster . . .

The SpaceSpider starts to rise up!
Higher!
High –
'Greetings, Pops!'
'Rocks! I wasn't expecting you this early. It's only just
got dark.'
   'Wow! Look at the SpaceSpider! It's floating! You doing that?

Course you are! Silly question! Amazing — Wait, Pops! You're stepping into the SpaceSpider! Woooow! It's carrying you! Like a surfboard. Only there's no surf. Just air! Where are you going, Pops?'

'Out of the window, Rocks.'

'Can see that. But why, Pops? What's happening? You sound different. Voice is . . . well, spooky. You know? What's happening, Pops? Why you wearing the accordion?'

'Listen to me, Rocky! I thought it was enough for us to meet in dreams. But I was wrong. I want us to meet in the real world too. And if your mum has her way, that will never be possible for us.'

'So . . . what you going to do?'

'You'll see —'

'Pops! Wait! Where you going? Wow! You can really ride this thing! It's whizzing down the street . . . Wait, Pops! Pops! Out across the wasteground . . . I can barely keep up with you —'

'Go home, Rocks!'

'No! I want to — Wow! Look at you move! Ride that SpaceSpider, Pops! It should be an Olympic sport! There's the Nuclear Power Plant! You're heading straight for it! Oh, what are you doing, Pops —?'

Don't let him distract you!

I know, I know.

Concentrate!

I'm trying! Now . . . land the SpaceSpider on the roof. There! Careful! Careful!

'Pops! Tell me —'

'Shut up, Rocks! You mustn't interfere with this!'

'But what is . . . this?'

I'm staring at the distant lights of Vinegar Street.

'Pops?'

My eyes get wider and wider.

'What you doing?'

My fingers press the keyboard . . .

I think of No. 7.
Concentrate!
Mandy Nylon!
Focus!
SPPIDDERRRSSS!!

And the spiders of Vinegar Street hear!
And they start to crawl!
Crawl towards . . .

Mandy is admiring her reflection in the dressing table mirror.

'People of Vinegar Ssstreet,' she says, rehearsing a speech she anticipates giving tomorrow, 'the kipper and vindaloo weirdosss of No. 1 have gone! The ssstreet is now oursss! Oh, I know sssome of you were friendsss of the weirdosss, and might have a tinge of regret at their departing, but there was no choice! Weirdosss hold usss back! Weirdosss stop usss having pretty gardensss and magnolia housssesss! Weirdosss are the enemies of all normal ssstreetsss –'

A noise!

Something rustling!

Mandy looks round the room.

Can't see anything.

Mandy resumes her speech –

'Weirdosss think they can wear what they like and talk how they like and be friendsss with who they –'

Rustle!

Louder this time.

What *is* that?

Slowly, Mandy stands and prowls round the room –

Rustle! Rustle!

It's coming from under the bed.

Mandy takes a stiletto off and prepares to strike whatever it is –

She gets to her knees and looks under –

A spider!

It dashes out and –

Splat!

The stiletto strikes.

'Got you!'

Then –

Another spider.

Splat!

'Got –'

Another.

Splat!

Another!

Another!

'Oh my . . .'

Twenty spiders!

Thirty spiders!

Like a black lava, spilling across the floor.

Mandy lashes out with her stiletto.

But it's no good.

The spiders just keep coming!

Huge, hairy spiders!

'Help!'

Mandy backs out of the bedroom!

She makes a dash for Rocky's bedroom but –

Spiders are dropping from the ceiling like black rain.

'Noooo!!'

Mandy backs down the stairs!

Spiders crawl after her!

Spiders on the ceiling!

She puts her stiletto on and dashes to the front door.

That's when a huge spider – with legs like hairy fingers – falls into her hair!

'HELPPPPPP!' cries Mandy, scarpering from the house. 'HELLL–'

That's my mum! I can hear her from here. What you up to, Pops? What's the music doing? Why did you yell, "Spiders!" like that? Look at your eyes! So big! Staring! You're scaring me, Pops! Stop it! I might not be able to stay here much longer. If I can hear Mum screaming from this distance, she'll probably –

– wake me up!'

No!

I'm back in my room!

And – yes! The door's still locked! Oh, Pops! Pops! Mum's in the street! Still screaming! I think she's rushing next door to –

Bruiser is sitting at the kitchen table, writing a letter:

Dear DeputieFudge and DeputiePops –
I dunno why you are being so darned pig-headed about DeputyMandie. She's the best darned thang to happen to this streat

since Old Gal first galloped me here. She says such nice thangs all the time. Nowun has ever made me feel such a healthy thuroughbred.

Why don't you give her a try? I'm sure you'd both look darned prerty with ya hair dun properly. Saddle sores 'n' spur blisters! You won't even need to wear a wig like me! Just a tuch of peroxide to liten it a little. And tight fitting dresses would soot you bofe just fine. And if you wore the right sort of bra

'Helppp!'
That sounds like –
Knock! Knock!
'Misss Bruiser!'
Bruiser opens the door and Mandy staggers in –
'SHUT IT, MISSS BRUISER! QUICK!'
Slam!
'You're making your hair as messy as a tumbleweed, Miss Mandy, clawing at it like that –'
'There'sss a ssspider in it!'
'A spid– Let me see! Here it is!'
'Drop it!'
Splat!
'Suffering cactus, Miss Mandy, what a darned fuss to make over a spider –'
'*A* ssspider! It'sss not jussst *a* ssspider. Look out of your window!'
'What do you –? Well, let's see! Mmm, mmm. Can't see anything!'
'Let me sssee! Why . . . you're right! It'sss totally dark!'
'Can't even see the geraniums and marigolds.'

'Oh no! No! You know why we can't sssee anything, Misss Bruiser?'

'Why?'

'AHHHHH –'

No use screaming! thinks Poppy. It's only just beginning!

What next?

FRROGGGS!

Croak!

'What'sss that?' gasps Mandy.

'It's coming from the back door!'

'Is it open?'

'Sure is! Summer nights are so hot –'

'Close it, Misss Bruissser! Quick!'

Bruiser rushes to the kitchen and –

Croak!

Croak!

'Suffering cactus!'

The floor is green with frogs!

From oven to table!

Jumping from fridge to oven!

Hundreds of them!

'Don't panic, Miss Mandy!' Bruiser tells Mandy. 'Just back down the hall – Wobbling wagonwheels! There's frogs up the stairs! And there! Spiders coming through the letterbox!'

'Hellllpppp!'

'Into the living room! Quick! I'll open this darned window! Spiders and frogs not here yet! Climb out! That's it! Now me – Darned difficult in this dress! – Watch out, Miss Mandy! A frog in your hair!'

'Get it out, Misss Bruissser! Quick!'

'Keep still! There! And look! There's spiders and frogs everywhere!'

Crash!

'They're knocking things over!'

Smash!

'And breaking windows – Quick! Run! Ruunnn – We'll go to Deputy Larry's.'

That's Bruiser's voice! And I can still hear Mum screaming! And things breaking! Oh, I've got to get out! Try the door! Push against the door! Won't budge! Perhaps I should have built up my muscles after all! . . . Look out of the window! Can't climb out! Too dangerous! Oh, Pops! Pops! Can you hear my thoughts? Rocks to Pops! Come in, Pops! Come in –

'*Come in.*'

I hear you, Rocks!

'*Wow! I can hear you too now! The music must give you such power –*'

What do you want?

'*You have to stop, Pops! The street's full of screaming and breaking! I'm sure Mum's learned her lesson.*'

I don't think so.

'*But –*'

I can't talk to you now, Rocks!

Can't listen to him any more!

Can't let anything interfere.
What next?
RAATTTS!

Squeak!
'Hear that, Misss Bruiser?' asks Mandy.
'Sounds like –'
'Amongssst the flowersss! Look!'
'Oh, no! Rats!'
Mandy knocks on Uncle Larry's door.
Bruiser knocks on Uncle Larry's door.
'Open up, Mr Larry!'
'Open up, DeputyLarry!'
Squeak!
Squeak!
'MR LARRY!!'
'DEPUTY –

– LARRY!'
Wow! Listen to that! Never heard Mum sound so scared. And I'm sure I heard rats! And look! Spiders crawling into my room now! Have to get out somehow! I know! Perhaps . . . perhaps FudgeMa can hear me! If I call out of the window!
'FUDGEMA!'
Nothing.

'FUDGEMA!'

Fudge's eyes click open.

'FUDGEMA!'

'Someone calling me – ooo!' she mutters to herself. 'Never the voice heard before . . . Who? Look window out of –'

'FUDGEMA!'

'YES – OOO? THAT WHO IS IT?'

'IT'S ROCKY! MANDY'S SON! IN THE HOUSE OPPOSITE! I'M LOCKED IN MY ROOM! YOU'VE GOT TO LET ME OUT –!'

'WHAT GOING ON –?'

'QUICK, FUDGEMA!'

Larry is spread out on his sofa. He's drunk one too many cocktails (despite promising Mandy he'd never touch the stuff again) and is mumbling –

'Oh, Fudgeducks! . . . Poppyducks! Please change your minds – please stop cooking pongy food . . . even though I love it, of course . . . Miss you if you leave . . . miss you so very much –'

BANG!

He jumps from the sofa.

'What's . . . what's that? Someone kicking at my door –'

'Open up, DeputyLarry!'

'Open up, Mr Larry!'

'Bruiserducks! Mandyducks! Don't say they looked through the window and caught me drinking! Oh, dear oh dear! Where's my wig –?'

BANG!

'I'M COMING!'

He rushes to the door and opens it.

'My cocktails are purely medicinal –'

'Shut the door, Mr Larry! Quick!'

Slam!

'Shut the windows, Mr Larry! Lock them and – Ahhhh!'

'Wh . . . what, Mandyducks?'

Mandy and Bruiser back away from Larry, pointing at his head.

For, in his haste, he hasn't picked up his wig.

It is a rat!

Squeak!

'AHHHHHHHH!'

'Sounds SweetieLarry like – ooo!' Fudge struggles into her dressing gown and peeks into Poppy's room. 'SweetiePops not in bed! . . . Oh, must rush . . . oooo . . . Look! Street spiders full of . . . And frogs . . . Rats – What going on is –?'

'FUDGEMA!'

'Coming – ooo – Rocky!' Careful cross street . . . Look! Oooo! The animals part! Open in front of up me! Don't hurt me want to – ooo! 'Coming – ooo – Rocky! Com – ing!'

'Hurry, FudgeMa!'

Oh, listen to the noises in the street! Frogs croaking! Rats squeaking! Spiders crawling! Things breaking and shattering! And the screaming –

'AHHHHH!!!' screams Mandy.

'AHHHHH!!!' screams Bruiser.

'AHHHHH!!!' screams Larry.

'Out, everyone!' yells Bruiser. 'Back door! Quick!'

And they scarper down the hall and open the back door and rush towards –

No. 4. The empty house. So you think you can escape me there, eh? Think its magnolia walls and marigolds will protect you?

They're terrified!

Good!

Don't you think that's enough?

Enough?! I haven't even started.

What next?

You'll see.

And Poppy pumps the accordion harder.

And fingers the keyboard faster.

WEEEEDDDDSSS!

A weed bursts through the grass!
  'Wobbling wagonwheels!'
  'Darned frightful!'
  'Ahhhhh!'
  Another weed.
  'Wobbling –'
  'Darned –'
  'Ahh –'
  Another weed!
  Another!
  And the weeds keep on growing.
  And growing . . .
  Growing.
  Weeds big as trees.
  Churning up the earth and wrapping themselves round
No. 4 Vinegar Street.
  Weeds break through windows!
  Smash!
  And break through the doors!
  Crash!

'NEXT HOUSE!' cries Bruiser. 'Quick! And mind the spiders – Ahhh!'

'Ahhhh!'

'Ahhhh!'

'And the rats! – Ahhhh!'

'Ahhhh!'

'Ahhhh!'
'And the weeds! – Ahhhh!'
'Ahhhh!'
'Ahhhh!'

Now I'm in – ooo – Mandy's house! Still the tiny animals for me part! How thoughtful of them –

'UPSTAIRS, FUDGEMA!'

'Coming, Rocky!'

'BACK ROOM, FUDGEMA!'

'Coming, Rocky! – Ooo! Are you in that room with – ooo – bolts on?'

'YES! THAT'S ME! TWO BOLTS! ONE AT TOP AND BOTTOM! LET ME OUT, FUDGEMA!'

Clunk!

Clunk!

'Greetings, FudgeMa!'

Bruiser tries the front door to No. 3.

Larry tries the window.

'Locked!'

'Bolted!'

'I'm going to Mr Harmony'sss houssse!' yells Mandy. 'That might be sssafe! Keep trying this houssse, though, people! Ahhh! The frogsss – Who knows where we'll need to hide – Ahhhh! Ratsss – Mr Harmony! MR HARMONY!'

But Mr Harmony can't hear a thing. He's tucked up in bed – with cotton wool in his ears – dreaming about ... money!

Oh, I'm going to make so much! Two new houses to sell! And when the weirdo Picklesticks move out –

'MR HARMONY!'

– I'll have yet another –

'MR HARMONY!'

– house to sell –

'MR HARMONY!'

Listen to that bonkers woman calling for Mr Harmony! But wait till she sees what I have for them next!

Don't get carried away.

I'm in complete control.

You don't look it.

Shut up! I've got to focus! And play! And –

BAAATTTSSS!

In the concrete corridors of the Nuclear Power Plant a million bats open their blood-red eyes . . .

And stretch their wings . . .

And fly . . .

'MR HARMONY! WAKE UP! IT'S MRSSS NYLON! –
What'sss that noissse? It sssounds like –'

Flap!
Flap!
Flap!
Flap!

'Look! It'sss a . . . big, black cloud! Getting clossser –'
FLAP!
FLAP!
'No – it'sss not a cloud! It's – AHHHHHHHH!!!'

'That's Mum! Oh, what can be happening – Careful,
FudgeMa! Don't tread on the spiders! Wait! They're
parting in front of us!'

'Everything does – ooo!'

'Wow! Of course! Pops wouldn't do anything to hurt
us!'

'SweetiePops? What do mean you – ooo?'

'Poppy's doing this, Fudge! Can't explain it all now!
But we've just got to stop her! Quick! To the street! That's
it! Wow! Look! Our house is covered with spiders. And
Bruiser's house is full of spiders and frogs. And Larry's
house is crawling with spiders and frogs and rats! And –
oh, look! You can't see No. 4 for weeds! And there's

Bruiser and Larry! Trying to get into No. 3. And Mum –
she's knocking at Mr Harmony's front door! And – oh,
WOOWW!! Look at the bats!'

'Ooooo!'

'They're swooping down and attacking Bruiser and
Larry –'

'Ahhhhhhh!'

'Ahhhhhh!'

Flap! Flap!

'Suffering cactuses! My wig's been plucked from my
head!'

'What dastardly creatures – Look! They've smashed the
windows of the house!'

'The darned bats are flying inside!'

'And the rats!'

'And the frogs!'

'And the spiders!'

'And – wobbling wagonwheels! – look at that! The
weeds are growing at Mandy's house!'

'And your house, Bruiserducks!'

'And your house, DeputyLarry!'

'MISS BRUISER! MR LARRY! COME HERE AND
HELP ME WAKE MR HARMONY! QUICK! QUICK!'

Mr Harmony is still dreaming of money. And building
new houses. Each one painted magnolia with a garden full
of geraniums and marigolds. Where everyone says, 'La-
de-dah' and is proud to live in his Community of
Harmony. Oh, yes! Oh, yes! Such a wonderful dream –
Zzzzzzzzzzz.

'WAKE UP, MR HARMONY!'
'WAKE UP, DEPUTYHARMONY!'
'WAKE UP, HARMONYDUCKS!'

'Wow! Look at the sky, Fudge! Clouds are whirling and swirling! There's a terrible storm on the way. And the whole street is becoming a cauldron of spiders, frogs, rats, weeds and bats. We've got to get out to the Nuclear Power Plant!'

'Why – ooo?'

'That's where Pops is! I've got to talk to her! Stop all this! Come on! We'll help the others wake Mr Harmony. Then we'll get him to drive us out to Poppy. That's the quickest way!'

Zzzzzz –

Enjoy the sleep while you can, baldy! You're about to wake in a nightmare –

You're *losing control*.

I'm not.

You are! Look at you.
I'm not.
But —

RUUBBBLLE!!!

A rumbling!
'What'sss that noissse, people?'
'Coming from the darned ground!'
'What dastardly thing is next?'
Rumbling gets louder.
Buildings start shaking.
'Oh, what'sss happening now, people?'
'SHE'S MAKING RUBBLE!' yells Rocky.
'You!' gasps Mandy, glaring at Rocky. 'How did you get
out?'

'I let him out – ooo!'

'Misss Fudge!'

'DeputyFudge!'

'Fudgeducks!'

'Go back to your room!' shrieks Mandy. 'Look at you! Showing me up in front of everyone with your weedy body.'

'DeputyMandy! What a terrible thing to say to your own son!'

'Frightfully nasty, Mandyducks!'

'DON'T YOU SEE!' Rocky shouts above the growing rumble. 'EVERYTHING POPPY TOLD YOU WAS RIGHT! AND YOU WOULDN'T BELIEVE HER! YOU LET HER DOWN! BETRAYED HER! THAT'S WHY POPPY'S DOING THIS –'

RUMBLE!

'Wobbling wagonwheels! Look! The houses are beginning to crumble – We've got to wake DeputyHarmony up! Quick! DEPUTYHARMONY!'

'HARMONYDUCKS!'

'MR HARMONY!'

'SWEETIEHARMONY!'

Zzzzzz!

Rumble.

Zzz –

'Stand back, everyone!' cries Rocky. 'I'm going to knock the door down! It's the only way . . . Take a few steps back . . . Now rush at it and –'

BUMFF!

'Ouch!'

Door doesn't budge.

'Wimp! My ssson is a wimp – Ahhh! No! Look! My houssse! It'sss falling down –'

The walls crash in at No. 7.

The ceiling falls through.

Spiders, frogs, rats and bats erupt from the tumbling building.

Dust billows up all round.

Rumble!

Crawl!

Croak!

Squeak!

Flap!

Weeds start growing amongst the ruins, slithering like snakes over shattered magnolia walls . . .

It's becoming my street again!

That's enough!

No!

But what else –?

Shut up!

Your fingers are moving so fast.

Yes! More music! More! More!

'I'll try Mr Harmony's door again!'

BUMFF – *split!*

'Wobbling wagonwheels! You're doing it, lad! The wood's giving way! Once more!'

Rocky steps back.

Then –

Rush.

And . . .

KRANGGG – CLUNK!

The door bursts open!

'Darned well done!'

'Bravo!'

'Ooo – yes!'

Rocky rushes inside –

Zzzzzz –

'Mr Harmony!'

Shake!

'MR HARMONY!'

'Wh – what! You! The unmacho son! What you doing here?'

'Get out of bed! Quick!'

'Wh– why?'

RUMBLE!

'Your house is falling down!'

♩

'Do you think he's all right in there, DeputyLarry?'
 'Oh, yes! What a brave young lad, Bruiserducks.'
 'Brave he is – ooo! And honest he is!'

RUMBLE!

'Oooo – SweetieBruiser! Look! Your house . . .'

The walls are crashing in at No. 6.
The ceiling falls through.
Spiders, frogs, rats and bats explode from the collapsing building.
Dust billows all round.
Rumble.
Crawl.
Croak!
Squeak!
Flap!
Weeds start growing among the ruins.

Is this what you wanted?
 I . . . I . . .

You're out of control! I told you. Stop now before it's too late.

'Misss Bruissser! Mr Larry! Mr Harmony! – Oh, look! Our ssstreet! What'sss happening? Ssspiders! Frogsss! Ratsss! Weedsss! Batsss! And – oh, look at you all! Hair a messs! Make-up sssmeared! Clothesss torn – Quick! Mr Harmony! Give me your car keysss!'

'My . . . car keys? But . . . they're in the house! On top of the fridge!'

'Then go and get them, Mr Harmony! Now!'
RUMBLE!

'I'm not going back in there, Mrs Nylon!'
RUMBLE! RUMBLE!

'I'll go,' says Rocky. 'We need the car to drive out to Pops.'

He dashes back into the house.

'Wobbling wagonwheels! If that ain't the bravest darn buck I've ever – DeputyLarry! Look! Your house!'

No. 5's walls are crumbling.

The ceiling falls through.

Spiders, frogs, rats and bats erupt from the collapsing building.

Dust billows all round.

Crawl.

Croak.

Squeak.

Flap.

Weeds grow!

Wow! Difficult to walk in here! Ground's trembling like jelly! But look! When things fall, they miss me! Oh, Pops! Your power won't hurt me, I know –

There!

The keys!

Grab them!

Back outside and –

'Give them to me, wimp!'

'But, Mum – we need the car to drive out to –'

'Are you crazy asss well asss wimpy? Go out there? Look what that little witch isss doing –'

'Don't call her a witch, Mum!'

'No! Don't, DeputyMandy!'

'No! Don't, Mandyducks!'
'No! Don't – oooo!'
'SHUT UP, PEOPLE! I'LL CALL HER WHAT I LIKE
...! Look round you. If thisss ain't witchcraft – Ahh!
Ssspiders up my legsss! – I don't know what isss! And you
want me to drive to her! – Ahh! Frogsss! – Never! Ahh!
Ratsss! – QUICK! MR HARMONY! LET'SSS HIDE IN
YOUR CAR!'

You can hide, you bonkers woman! But you can't escape!
Mercy me, no! Wherever you go, my music will find
you ...

'Wow! You hear that? Music!'
'It's – ooo – SweetiePops!'
'DeputyPops!'

'Poppyducks! – It's coming from everywhere! Filling the air! So beautiful and . . . oh, frightful!'

RUMBLE!

RUMBLE!

RUMBLE!

No. 4's walls crumble.
Ceiling falls.
Animals erupt from collapsing building.
Dust.
Crawl.
Croak.

Squeak.
Flap.
Weeds!

'What are we going to do? We need to get to Pops! Mum and Mr Harmony are in the car and –'

No. 3's walls crumble.
Ceiling falls.

Animals erupt.
Dust.
Weeds –

'Wow! The rumbling's getting louder! And the ground is shaking and shaking! And look! Mr Harmony's house –!'

No. 2's walls crumble.
'Wobbling wagonwheels! Stand back!'

Ceiling falls.
Spiders!
Frogs!
Rats!
Bats!
Dust.
FudgeMa coughs.
Bruiser coughs.
Larry coughs.
Rocky coughs then cries – 'HOW ARE WE GOING TO
GET TO POPS? IF WE CAN'T USE THE CAR –' cough,
cough – 'IT'LL TAKE TOO LONG TO WALK!'

'WE WON'T HAVE TO WALK!' Bruiser yells. 'QUICK!
TO NEW GAL!'

'Look at them run, Mr Harmony! What a messs they look! What a messs thisss ssstreet isss! I told you we ssshould've got rid of the weirdosss sssooner – Ahh! Frogs and spidersss on the windsssscreen! They can't get in, can they, Mr Harmony?'

'No, Mrs Nylon.'

'I hate it here now, Mr Harmony! Thisss will never be a Mandy Nylon sssort of ssstreet! – Ahhh! A ssspider's on your head! – Quick! Have you got a pen and paper?'

'Wh– why, Mrs Nylon?'

'I want to write a note . . .'

'Wobbling wagonwheels! There's New Gal. Clear the bricks off, everyone . . . That's it –'

FLASH!

BOOM!

'Wow! Listen to that! Thunder and lightning! It's started to rain! I've never seen a storm like it.'

Splash!

Splash!

'Suffering cactus! DeputyLarry! DeputyFudge! In the side-carriage – Oh, my! What's that?'

RUMBBBLLE!!

'It's a . . . Wow! It's a crack forming in the street! All the rumbling has caused it! An earthquake! And look! The crack's splitting, moving up the street . . . into the wasteground . . . Oh no! No! It's heading out to the Nuclear Power Plant. No! IF THE CRACK TOUCHES THE NUCLEAR POWER PLANT . . . IF IT CRACKS THAT CONCRETE –'

'Don't think about it, DeputyRocks! Sit behind me. Now – hang on, everyone! YEEEE-HAAAA!!!'

'Look at thisss note I've written, Mr Harmony.'
   'But Mrs Nylon –'
   'Jussst read!'

'DEAR PEOPLE –
I HAVE GONE AWAY WITH MR HARMONY.
AS FAR AS I'M CONCERNED YOU ARE
ALL A BUNCH OF HOPELESS LOSERS, AND
IF I NEVER SEE ANY OF YOU AGAIN IT'LL
BE TOO SOON.
  AS MY WIMPY SON SEEMS TO LIKE THE
VINDALOO WEIRDOS SO MUCH, HE CAN
STAY WITH THEM FROM NOW ON. PERHAPS
THEY'LL APPRECIATE HIS MUSCLELESS
BODY AND WEEDY VOICE.
  GOODBYE FOR EVER

  MANDY NYLON'

'Oh . . . Mrs Nylon –'

'Do you agree with it?'

'You bet your sweet patootie! You and me together! Oh, yes!'

'Then rush outsssside and ssstick it in No. 1's letterbox! Quick!'

'I will. But – wait! Just a little something I want to add!'

P.S. This is Mr Harmony! I don't want to see any of you sarcastic lot again either. This house is now the property of the Picklesticks! I'm going to build a new community with Mrs Nylon and fill it with tenants who don't give me ulcers!

Mr Harmony

'Agreed, Mrs Nylon?'

'Agreed, Mr Harmony. Now – oh, possst it and let'sss get out of here! Oh, the ssspiders! The frogsss! The ratsss! The batsss! And look at that huge crack in the ssstreet – Quick, Mr Harmony! Let's get out of here! Let's get out!'

Stop! You're out of control! Stop!
I'm . . . I'm trying. But –
But what?
I can't stop!
You must!
But I can't! I can't! I can't!

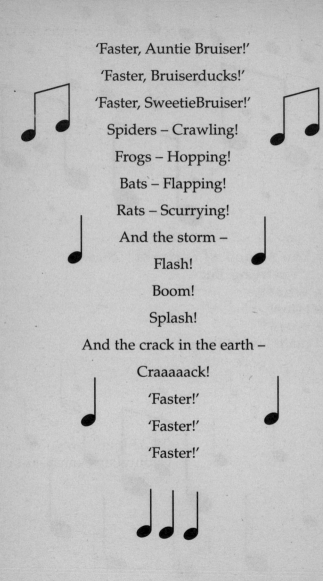

'Faster, Auntie Bruiser!'

'Faster, Bruiserducks!'

'Faster, SweetieBruiser!'

Spiders – Crawling!

Frogs – Hopping!

Bats – Flapping!

Rats – Scurrying!

And the storm –

Flash!

Boom!

Splash!

And the crack in the earth –

Craaaaack!

'Faster!'

'Faster!'

'Faster!'

'We're keeping up with it, Auntie Bruiser!'

'We've got to get ahead of it, Bruiserducks!'

'Quicker, SweetieBruiser!'

'Wobbling   wagonwheels! DeputyPops' music just gets louder –'

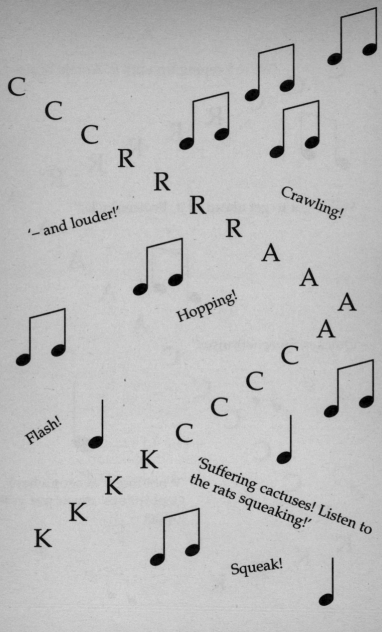

K
K
K
Squeak!

C
Boom!
R
R
A
'Faster! Faster!'
C
K
K

'That's it, Bruiser!'
'We're ahead, Bruiserducks!'
'Done well, SweetieBruiser!'
'Faster!'
'Faster!'
'Faster!'
'Pops! There she is!
Standing on top of
the building! POPS!
P
O
P
S
, S

That's Rocks! There he is! And FudgeMa! Uncle Larry! Auntie Bruiser! All of them splashed with mud! And – oh, what's that? A crack in the earth! Like a black serpent making its way towards –

No!

Extreme danger!

I know!

Stop!

Can't!

H
E
E
E
L
L
L
P
P
P
P
!

'Pops is in trouble!
Oh, look at her!
Her face is full of panic! –
We're here!
Stop the bike, Bruiser –
Get out!
Wow!
It's so muddy!'
Squelch!
Squelch!
Squelch!
'Stop the music, Pops!'
'Stop, DeputyPops!'
'Stop, Poppyducks!'
'Stop – ooo, SweetiePops!'
'I can't! I can't!
It just keeps playing!
Help!
HELLLPP!
HEELLPPP!'
'Pops!
Look!
The crack!
It's getting
closer
and
closer!'

C
C
C
R
R
R
A
A
A
C
C
K
K

'Wobbling wagonwheels!'
'Look! The crack!'
'Dastardly thing!'
'Ooooo!'
'Pops!'
'HELP!'
'STOP, POPS!'
'I CAN'T –'

'I'm climbing the ladder up to you, Pops!'

'Be careful, DeputyRocky!'

'Careful, Rockyducks!'

'Fullcare – ooo, SweetieRocky!'

'Wow! It's slippery!'

Raining heavier!

So many spiders!

And rats!

And bats!

Mud!!

'Pops!'

'Rocks!'

Careful . . . careful.

The wind's like a hurricane now!

And . . .

FLASSHHH!!!
BOOM!

Thunder!

Lightning!

Rain!

'Pops! It's like the sky's exploding!'

'HELP ME, ROCKS!'

Flap!

'Help, Rocks!'

'Wow!'

FLASSHHH!!!

Croak!

'Pops!'

'Pops!'

Boom!

'Rocks!'

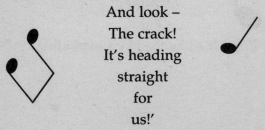

'You've got to stop the music, Pops! You know that!
There's hardly anything left of the street!
And look –
The crack!
It's heading
straight
for
us!'

CRRRAAACCCKKK

'If
it
splits
the concrete
on the Power Plant,
oh, Pops –
– it could be
the end of
the
world!'

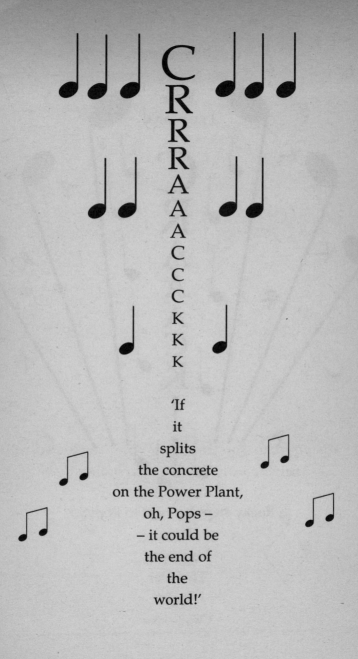

'Mercy me!
I want to stop, Rocks!
But –
I just can't!'

Rocky steps up next to Poppy.
Rain.
Lightning.
Thunder.
'Pops!'
'Oh, Rocks!'

Rocky leans forward and gives her –

A KISS!

And the music stops playing.
And the earth stops cracking.
And the ground stops rumbling.
And everyone stops screaming.
And the wind stops howling.
And the lightning stops flashing.
And the thunder stops booming.
And the rain stops lashing.
And spiders return to their webs.
And frogs return to their water.
And rats return to their lairs.
And bats return to their caverns.
And everything is still.
No more crawling.
No more hopping.
No more flapping.
No squeaking.
No croaking.
Peaceful.
Tranquil.
Silent.
Calm . . .

Epilogue

— 68 —

Later, Poppy and Rocky walk across the rubble.

They can hear FudgeMa, Auntie Bruiser and Uncle Larry laughing and joking inside the house.

'We're going to be happy now, Rocks. I can tell! One house – but full of such different people. Mercy me! How glorious! Oh, Auntie Bruiser and Uncle Larry are so sorry for what they did. They don't know what got into them. But I do. It was your mum. Well, she's gone now. It's just them and . . . and us. Me with you, Rocks.'

'And me with . . . you, Pops.'

They sit on a large piece of rubble and look up at the twilight sky where a few remaining stars still twinkle.

'We can astral travel, Pops.'

'We can, Rocks!'

'Fly through each other.'

'Oh, yes!'

'And – fly higher than ever.'

'Where are you thinking?'

'The moon?'

'Oh, why stop at the moon?' asks Poppy, staring into Rocky's eyes. 'Let's aim for Venus!'

That's quite romantic.

No wisecracks! I'm too happy.

Then I'm happy too.

You are?

Of course. After all, we're friends.

We are?
For ever and ever, kid.
Don't call me kid.

Scribbleboy

by Philip Ridley

'My name is Scribbleboy and I'm back to scribble!

Years ago, Scribbleboy had transformed the gloomy grey
concrete of the neighbourhood with his fabulous shapes and
colours . . . until, without warning, he vanished. Most of the
Scribbles were destroyed and only the Scribbleboy Fan Club
kept his legend alive.

Then, one night, a strange figure is seen and a mysterious voice
heard . . .

Could the impossible have happened?
Has the legend come true?
Is Scribbleboy really back?

'Ridley is a multi-talented purveyor of children's fiction with an
edge – sharp writing and even sharper characterization. Highly
recommended' – *Publishing News*

'Ridley is fast becoming a cult figure'
– Mary Hoffman, *Daily Telegraph*

Kasper in the Glitter

by Philip Ridley

For the first time in his life, Kasper opened the garden gate.

And stepped into The Nothing . . .

Kasper Whisky lives with his mother, Pumpkin, far away from The City. But the arrival of a boy called Hearthrob Mink changes Kasper's life for ever, taking him to The City and the enticing but dangerous world of King Streetwise.

'Philip Ridley is a wildly inventive and imaginative writer' – *Daily Telegraph*

'Pacey, punchy and refreshingly different' – *Young Telegraph*

'Witty, poignant, intelligent, absorbing . . . Ridley is the Pied Piper of contemporary children's fiction' – *Big Issue*

Meteorite Spoon

by Philip Ridley

Fergal dropped the meteorite spoon. Dust filled the air. Filly and Fergal were just about to shriek, when – CRASH!

No parents – not in The Whole History of Parents Arguing – argued as much as Filly and Fergal's parents.

When Mr and Mrs Thunder have the biggest argument of all time, they finally bring the house down! Trapped beneath the rubble, Filly and Fergal escape, with the help of the magical meteorite spoon, to a technicolour fantasy island, Honeymoonia. Can this extraordinary world really be true? Are the glamorous Mr and Mrs Love really a young version of Mum and Dad? And what happens when the volcano erupts?

Expect the unexpected as award-winning Philip Ridley takes you on a weird and wonderful adventure.

'Ridley has to be Dahl's successor' – *Books for Keeps*

ZinderZunder

by Philip Ridley

Dear none too happy young person, my name is ZinderZunder and I can give you want you want ...

Mumzie wants Max to be a little gentleman. Max wants Mumzie to stop criticizing him and realize just how fabulously razzmatazz his tap-dancing is. Can ZinderZunder make Max's wish come true?

'Philip Ridley tells this ultra-modern morality tale of tap-dancing Max with showman skill' – Jacqueline Wilson

'Ridley has to be Dahl's successor' – *Books for Keeps*

'One of the outstanding new writers for older children' – *Sunday Times*

Dakota of the White Flats

by Philip Ridley

Dakota wanted to run but couldn't move. It's going to kill me! she thought. Then a hand landed on Dakota's shoulder. 'Got you, darling,' hissed Medusa.

When Dakota Pink decides to find out the truth about Medusa's baby monster it is the beginning of a quest that will lead Dakota and her best friend Treacle away from the White Flats to Dog Island and the Fortress. Will they manage to escape the mutant killer eels to discover what lies behind the barbed wire of the Fortress and who the mysterious Lassitter Peach is?

Award-winning author Philip Ridley takes his readers on a rollercoaster of an adventure full of thrills and surprises.

'Ridley looks set to be one of the outstanding new writers for older children' – *Sunday Times*

READ MORE IN PUFFIN

For children of all ages, Puffin represents quality and variety – the very best in publishing today around the world.

For complete information about books available from Puffin – and Penguin – and how to order them, contact us at the appropriate address below. Please note that for copyright reasons the selection of books varies from country to country.

On the worldwide web: www.puffin.co.uk

In the United Kingdom: Please write to *Dept. EP, Penguin Books Ltd, Bath Road, Harmondsworth, West Drayton, Middlesex UB7 ODA*

In the United States: Please write to *Consumer Sales, Penguin USA, P.O. Box 999, Dept. 17109, Bergenfield, New Jersey 07621-0120*. VISA and MasterCard holders call 1-800-253-6476 to order Penguin titles

In Canada: Please write to *Penguin Books Canada Ltd, 10 Alcorn Avenue, Suite 300, Toronto, Ontario M4V 3B2*

In Australia: Please write to *Penguin Books Australia Ltd, P.O. Box 257, Ringwood, Victoria 3134*

In New Zealand: Please write to *Penguin Books (NZ) Ltd, Private Bag 102902, North Shore Mail Centre, Auckland 10*

In India: Please write to *Penguin Books India Pvt Ltd, 706 Eros Apartments, 56 Nehru Place, New Delhi 110 019*

In the Netherlands: Please write to *Penguin Books Netherlands bv, Postbus 3507, NL-1001 AH Amsterdam*

In Germany: Please write to *Penguin Books Deutschland GmbH, Metzlerstrasse 26, 60594 Frankfurt am Main*

In Spain: Please write to *Penguin Books S. A., Bravo Murillo 19, 1º B, 28015 Madrid*

In Italy: Please write to *Penguin Italia s.r.l., Via Felice Casati 20, I–20124 Milano*

In France: Please write to *Penguin France S. A., 17 rue Lejeune, F–31000 Toulouse*

In Japan: Please write to *Penguin Books Japan, Ishikiribashi Building, 2–5–4, Suido, Bunkyo-ku, Tokyo 112*

In South Africa: Please write to *Longman Penguin Southern Africa (Pty) Ltd, Private Bag X08, Bertsham 2013*